THE PRINCIPLES

A Novel

Also by this author

Barry Cameron has also written
The ABC's of Financial Success

and (with Douglas J. Crozier)

The ABC's of Financial Success Workbook
with accompanying CD-ROM

Both are available from HeartSpring Publishing
www.heartspringpublishing.com
A division of College Press Publishing Co.
www.collegepress.com

THE PRINCIPLES
A Novel

Barry L. Cameron & Tom Pryor

HEARTSPRING PUBLISHING · JOPLIN, MISSOURI

© 2003 by Barry L. Cameron & Tom Pryor

Published by HeartSpring Publishing
a division of College Press Publishing Company
www.collegepress.com
Toll-free order line 800-289-3300

Printed and bound in the
United States of America

Unless otherwise noted, Scripture quotations are taken from
THE HOLY BIBLE, NEW INTERNATIONAL VERSION®. NIV®.
Copyright © 1973, 1978, 1984, by International Bible Society.
Used by permission of Zondervan Publishing House.
All rights reserved.

This book is a work of fiction. Certain locations, products, and public figures may be mentioned, but are used fictitiously. All other characters, events, and dialogue described in the book are totally imaginary. Any resemblance to actual persons, living or dead, events, or locales, is entirely coincidental.

Cover design by Mark A. Cole

ISBN 0-89900-068-1

Dedications

To the Author and Perfector of our faith, Jesus Christ.

To the best co-author, friend, and pastor
I could ever ask for, Barry Cameron.

To four women who played important roles
in giving birth to this book: my wife Sue,
my staff member, Christine Nola,
Barry's assistant, Vicki Dietz,
and writer Darlene Brinker.

Tom

To the thousands of Christian men and women
who are making their mark on the marketplace
for Jesus Christ every day.

To our staff, elders, and our entire
Crossroads Christian Church family.

Barry

Acknowledgements

To our families for their patience while we completed the arduous task of putting *The Principles* on paper.

To those who have already embraced Activity Based Management and have seen that *The Principles* really do work.

To Vicki Dietz, Barry's assistant, for making us look better than we are.

To Dru Ashwell, our friend and editor at HeartSpring.

1

As Ray Miller cradled the phone on his shoulder and typed a few keys on the computer, a spreadsheet appeared on the monitor. Glancing at the picture of Gloria and the kids on his desk, he said, "Honey, I'm really sorry. I know, but I'm still working on this report for tomorrow. Just go ahead and eat without me."

Ray sighed as he hung up and turned his attention to the screen. His heart sank. Megna Electronics' profits had fallen short of corporate goals for five months running, and this past month's results were no better. As the company's controller, it was his job to present the monthly accounting report, and he hated to be the bearer of bad news once again. Sorting through all the other data his staff had pulled together—sales reports, cost analyses, and departmental budgets—he tried to think about ways he could present the material, as if the sheer quantity of information could somehow camouflage the sorry news. He combed through the numbers for something positive to say, or even for ways to explain Megna's disappointing performance. There were tons of data but not much to work with.

Ray stretched and rubbed his eyes. He called the deli downstairs and ordered a chicken sandwich and a Coke. It looked like he wasn't even going to get home in time to see the kids before bed.

At this point in his career it wasn't supposed to be like this. He'd spent many late nights crunching numbers in the past; he'd accepted them as a part of paying his dues. Fifteen years ago, fresh out of Wharton Business School, he had fully expected to make a real contribution to the world of business someday, but he had understood even then that he needed to master the details before he would be able to make a difference.

Many of his business school friends had gone into investment banking or corporate finance, and some of them had made a pile of money over the years. Accounting wasn't regarded as the most glamorous profession, but he believed strongly that managing a business required having an understanding of its financial underpinnings. If the object of any business was to make money, then understanding a company's finances would help keep it on track and growing. Sure, he expected to earn enough to live in a nice home, send his kids to college, and enjoy some of the finer things in life; that's why he'd gone to business school in the first place. But he also had this idea that it would be satisfying simply to help make a company successful.

Ray felt he had been trained well at Arthur Andersen, his first job out of business school. There were certainly late nights then, but it was exciting to help audit the records of companies whose names were household words. And later, after he had switched over to the corporate side of the business, he had enjoyed learning to be as good a manager as he was an accountant. His staff respected him, and the accounting department had gained a reputation for thoroughness, accuracy, and on-time delivery.

But now, after eight years at Megna Electronics, the thrill was definitely gone. As controller he had plenty of responsibility, corporate visibility, and a boss he liked and respected. Ray was well paid, received generous benefits, and got four weeks of vacation every year. He should be content, but the work itself had become stale. Looking at his ninety-sixth financial review on the screen in front of him, he wondered how it could possibly benefit anyone. Here he was, mechanically cranking out a report that would have no more impact than the ones before it, and he was shortchanging his family to boot.

Before he and Gloria had married, the trade-offs hadn't been so great. Gloria was working then and often had to stay late at the office, too, and there were no kids to disappoint. Sometimes they would meet at a restaurant, briefcases in hand, for a late-night supper and then trade stories about the day. Gloria told great stories—mostly stories that made him laugh. But she was also a great listener and would give him her complete attention as he described a meeting with his boss or shared some office gossip.

That seemed like a long time ago. Now evenings were full of soccer practice and science projects, which were fine, but there wasn't much time to just sit and talk. He had once tried to describe his frustration with work to Gloria, but she hadn't even had a chance to listen as she was busy too.

Ray was glad, he guessed, that his salary allowed them to live comfortably enough without Gloria's paycheck. She had wanted to stay home to raise the kids, and for the most part, that had worked well. They lived on a shady street in one of the top school districts in Texas. Gloria managed the household well and kept them all clean, fed, and organized. They belonged to an exclusive country club. They weren't really the country club type, but Ray loved to golf and Gloria played tennis, so it seemed worth the money. He thought they had just about everything they needed.

But Ray had to admit that sometimes he felt burdened with the pressure of being the sole breadwinner. Job security had become much more important to him than he had ever expected, and when you're afraid to take risks, things can get a little dull. Then again, even if his job had become a little monotonous, it at least paid the bills. Maybe he'd just have to wait to do something truly important until after the kids finished college.

In the meantime, one could see all the signs of Ray's success at work: his corner office looked out over Megna's beautifully landscaped grounds, and beyond them you could see the city skyline. There was a round glass table for when small groups came to meet with him and a "power" desk and leather chair that had been a gift when he was promoted. One wall was lined with management and accounting books, and an oversized greaseboard was mounted on another.

The greaseboard was Ray's favorite thing about the office; it had been ordered according to his specifications and had become his trademark. Almost every meeting with Ray included the squeak of his marker on the board. It was how he kept his thoughts straight. Tonight, however, the greaseboard was blank, reflecting Ray's mind regarding the monthly accounting report.

His sandwich arrived. Ray tipped the delivery boy and started to unwrap his dinner. Then he changed his mind. Who was he fooling? He wasn't going to get any more done tonight. He'd just have to come in a little early tomorrow, fix a few charts, and wing it at the meeting. He picked up the phone and called Gloria. "I'm on my way home."

2

Ray was surprised to see his boss's car already in the parking lot as he pulled in at 7:30 the next morning. John Brady was such an unflappable leader that it was rarely apparent he was under much pressure. John's job was to turn Megna's profits around, but profits had lagged now for months on end. John was smart, decisive, and fair, everything you'd want in a good boss. At fifty, he still had the energy and drive of a young manager, but he also had the experience of a seasoned executive. He picked good people to manage the business, and Megna had an impressive lineup of quality products. So why was the company doing so poorly?

John was on a conference call as Ray went past his office—probably headquarters ragging on him about the monthly profit report. But Ray didn't have time to worry about John's problems. He needed to find a rabbit to pull out of his hat.

An hour later, armed with his report—but no rabbit—Ray entered the conference room. Nearly all the department managers had already taken their seats, most with their own overheads. As usual, Ray turned on the projector and put his "overview" chart up. There, in bright lights on the big screen, were this month's miserable profits and losses for all to see.

Ray pointed to the profit line on the screen. "As you can see, we missed the March pretax profit plan by $5.3 million."

"That's clear as day, Ray, but what we need to know is *why*. Why did we miss the plan? What can we do to get back on track?" John Brady's voice had an unfamiliar edge that made Ray uneasy.

Ray cleared his throat. "I was about to get to that, John." He paused, then plunged right in, knowing full well that he had not found a decent answer last night or this morning. "While sales were good this month, our costs exceeded budget primarily due to several things. First, we had an unfavorable raw material purchase price variance. Second, we had an unfavorable swing in manufacturing burden absorption, partially offset by deferred overhead expenditures. Finally, we—"

"Stop right there, Ray. Is there anyone at this table who can help me out by translating what Ray just said? Because frankly, Ray, not a word you've said means a thing to me." John picked up the financial report in front of him and let it drop with a thud. "Every month we get mind-numbing figures that don't do a thing to help us improve. Our company is sick, Ray. We need a diagnosis, not anesthetics."

The attack seemed to come out of nowhere. Ray suspected John's phone call this morning had something to do with his reaction. Trying to remain calm, he took a deep breath. "John, I can't change what the numbers say. My staff works very hard to give you an accurate account of the month's performance."

John leaned forward to reply. "That's just it, Ray. I'm not questioning the accuracy of the data. I know you work hard, and I'm sure your explanation of our poor performance is technically correct. But these accounting reports are precisely useless. They're precise, but they don't help us run the business. We need something from you that's approximately relevant! I'm either happy or sad each month, but never smarter. The monthly accounting reports are old news by the time I get it. They tell me *what* happened forty days ago. I need to know *why*. If I don't know why things happened, I can't recommend a solution."

Ray started to pull out some more charts, as if there might be answers in the other data he had prepared. John abruptly stood up, yanked the overhead plug from the outlet and said loudly, "Ray, you're drowning us in data. I don't need more data; I need information!" Everyone sat motionless. No one had ever seen John Brady lose his cool in a meeting.

Glancing to his left, John asked, "Chuck, am I off base here? Does anyone in this room agree with what I just said?"

"Oh, great," fumed Ray. Chuck Anderson had run the manufacturing department for twelve years. By the time Ray joined Megna, Chuck had his systems firmly in place, and he had no intention of making any changes. Chuck regarded the accounting staff as an annoyance that had to be tolerated. Providing information to Ray's staff was clearly a waste of his valuable time. In meetings it seemed like he always had something negative to say.

Chuck cleared his throat. "Well, I have to say I agree with you one hundred percent, John. Our accounting reports are just like the barometric pressure on the Channel 5 TV News. 'Precisely useless,' as you say." He looked around the table. "Every night the weatherman says something like, 'The barometric pressure today is 29.97 and rising.' But so what? Just because it has decimal points, it's supposed to be useful information? Is 29.97 good or bad? I don't know. What do I do if it's 29.97 and rising? Run for a storm shelter or plan a picnic?"

Before Ray could respond, Dick Conway from Engineering chimed in. "I have to agree with Chuck. These accounting reports don't help us either. Ray's people can tell me to the fourth decimal point how much direct labor it takes to produce each one of our products, but they can't tell my design engineers how many dollars of procurement or order fulfillment costs are consumed by a particular product." Ray's heart sank. Dick's reputation as a straight shooter, one who could cut through the clutter and home in on the important facts, made everyone take what he said very seriously. Several other managers began to speak at once.

"Okay, okay, everybody." To Ray's relief, John had calmed down and was taking control of the meeting again. "Listen, Ray, I'm sorry I lost my temper. Pulling the plug on you was inappropriate and not meant personally. But it is appropriate for us to look carefully at what our accounting system is doing, or not doing, for us."

Ray nodded at the apology but had nothing to say. He sat down. John went on. "Ray, no one can dispute the accuracy of your reports. I know you're a hard worker with a staff of great people. I also know from the corporate audit department that you are in compliance with every rule in the book. And that's great! But our accounting reports should also help us to plan, control, and make tough decisions. They don't, and that's the real issue here."

John got up again, but this time he walked over to a credenza on the far side of the room. He picked up a handful of blank paper and continued. "Let's try a little experiment I learned at the conference I went to last week."

He walked around the table and handed each person a blank piece of paper.

"Ray, I want you to rate our accounting system with a number from one to ten. A one means the system does a poor job of meeting our business needs, and a ten means it's outstanding. Just write your number down on the paper." Ray thought for a few moments and then wrote down his number.

"Good," said John. "Now I want everyone else to do the same. Rate how well our accounting system meets your department's needs. Ten is terrific and one is useless. Remember, you are rating the system, not Ray or his staff. I'll do the same. When everyone is finished, pass me your sheets. Ray, you hold on to yours."

Everyone thought for a few seconds, wrote down a number, and passed the sheets to John. John listed every response except Ray's on a flipchart. Chuck rated it a 4. So did Dick and most of the others. Two of them were a little more generous and wrote down 5. Adding his own 3, John calculated in his head that the average was about 4.

"Okay, Ray, what's your number?"

Ray tried not to sound defensive. "I gave it a 7.5."

"Ray, somehow I knew you'd be the one with a decimal point in the rating." Everyone, even Ray, chuckled. "Okay. Now Ray here, representing the accounting department, gave our system a 7.5." He paused, getting more serious. "But the people who use these reports gave it a 4."

"You're all overreacting," said Ray. "Missing the budget and profit plan is no reason to bash the accountants."

"You're missing the point, Ray. It's not the accountants. It's the accounting system that's the problem. I agree we shouldn't overreact, but we can't just sit here and do nothing, hoping the numbers will look better next month. As my grandmother used to say, 'Hope is not a method of improvement.' We've got to do something here. We need some relevant and useful information to make decisions, reduce costs, and increase profits."

"Well, what *do* you want us to do?" Ray said, flustered. He didn't know what else he could say.

John looked around the table again. "For starters, let's list some of the reasons we rated the accounting system so low. If we can identify the problem, maybe we can come up with a solution." He walked over to the flipchart and wrote Happy or Sad P&L. "I'll start," said John.

"My biggest beef with the system is that it reports variances to the budget after they have already happened. This month is a good example. We had unfavorable variances to the budget. My boss is sad. I'm sad. You're sad. We're all sad. I want to be happy. Based on what you said earlier, we really don't know the root causes for the variances. I need a system that either prevents the variance or lets me know early enough so that I can do something to solve the problem. I don't want variances. Instead I want something that *prevents* variances.

Ray nodded "Yes, but how?"

John looked around and asked, "Does anyone else have an issue to add before we brainstorm some solutions?"

Chris Meyers from Sales looked sympathetically at Ray and raised his hand. Everyone liked Chris. He was smart, funny, and had a way of putting people at ease.

John looked at him thoughtfully for a moment and then said, "Before you give me your two cents, Chris, I want to know where you got that tie." Everyone laughed. Chris's ties were legendary, and today he was wearing one with a subtle red and black pattern, which, on close examination, turned out to be red and black dollar signs.

Chris grinned. "You know I never reveal my sources," he said. "I just thought it was appropriate for our P&L meeting."

John just shook his head. "Okay, so what did you want to add to the list?"

"Well, could we add Financial Biorhythm to the list?" Chris

asked. "Our current system causes us to ship fifty percent of our sales orders in the last week of every month. I know for a fact that fifty percent of the orders don't come in then. I wonder what would happen if we eliminated our policy of closing the accounting books monthly."

Chuck interrupted. "You're right, Chris. Last week I had a forklift driver in the warehouse stop and ask me if it was month-end. His question caught me off guard. At first I thought he was illiterate and couldn't read a calendar. But then it hit me—he wanted to know if it was the end of the accounting month and, sure enough, it was!"

Chris continued, "That's exactly what I mean, Chuck. It seems to me that every department at Megna builds up momentum during the month, blows it out the last week, and then starts the process all over again the first week of the next month. I bet if we tracked our quality defects on a calendar, we would find most of them in the first and last week of every month. I think we need hourly or daily performance measures, not monthly after-the-fact measurements."

Ray smiled. "I'm all for that one. I'd love to stop monthly closing and switch to a quarterly process. That would free up a lot of time for my staff to do other work. But I don't think corporate headquarters would ever approve that. Do you, John?"

John quickly responded, "Let's not get into a discussion of solutions just yet. We'll do that later. Now, does anyone else have something for our list?"

"I have one," Vince Larkin from Quality Control entered the discussion. Ray liked Vince and had always attributed his down-to-earth manner to the fact that he had taught sixth-grade science before coming to Megna. "Add 'Stupid Budget Questions' to the list. Every three months I'm asked to create a twelve-month expense budget for my department. I submit it to Ray's staff, and then they set up a meeting for you to review it, John. And no offense, but you ask some pretty stupid questions during that session. And I know you're not a stupid person, John."

"Thank you," said John, amused, as everyone else laughed. "I'll take any compliments I can today."

"Go ahead and laugh," Vince continued, "but it's true. John doesn't ask about the cost of quality, customer satisfaction issues, or process improvement plans during my budget review. Instead, he asks me, 'How many trips do you have in your travel budget?' or 'Have you negotiated a lower-cost vendor for testing supplies?' John, am I talking out of turn here, or do you agree that our current budget and accounting system forces us to ask—and answer—stupid questions."

John laughed. "I have to admit it . . . you're right, Vince. Especially the part about my not being stupid."

Ray was beginning to relax. At least John wasn't accusing him personally and was taking some of the heat himself. And Ray did see some truth in the issues that had been raised so far. But fixing things would be another matter.

Mary Forsman from Human Resources raised her hand. Mary had been Ray's first contact at Megna, years ago, and although they'd had disagreements over the years, he respected her. She was in her sixties, though she seemed much younger. She wore her red hair up in a French twist and seemed to have an endless supply of interesting earrings to match her outfits. Mary had been with the company forever. Ray often relied on her as a voice of experience.

"John," began Mary, "I have another one for your list. Add Yesterday's Newspaper."

John nodded as he wrote it down. "Go ahead, Mary. Please explain."

"How many of you would pay me a dollar for yesterday's *Wall Street Journal*?" No one responded. "No one wants old news. Yet our monthly accounting report is exactly that. It's thirty-five-day-old news. My guess is we're paying a lot of money for that old news."

John turned to Ray. "How much does it cost to prepare the monthly financial report?"

Ray shrugged. "I don't know, John. I wouldn't even venture a guess."

Mary continued. "Based on conversations with members of

Ray's accounting staff, we spend an enormous amount of overtime creating yesterday's news."

Great. The boss is mad, my colleagues hate my work, and now it sounds like my own staff is complaining to Human Resources, thought Ray.

John glanced at his watch. They had already spent more time than he had planned discussing the accounting system. "Before we wrap this up, should we add anything else to our list?"

Mark Paley, the materials manager, had been listening quietly to the discussion but now said, "How about adding 'The Usual Suspects' to the list? For example, when our profits are not what headquarters wants, it seems John always asks Ray to round up the usual suspects. Ray gets all the managers in a room, tells us to freeze spending, stop travel, cancel training, and lay off some of our workers. A ten percent across-the-board budget cut might be equal, but it's certainly not fair. It assumes that everyone has the same amount of discretionary budget or waste. But freezing spending or eliminating workers does nothing to affect the root causes of our costs."

"I think you're making a good point," said John, "but can you give us an example?"

Mark thought for a moment. "Think of cost-cutting as mowing the lawn. Based on your request, John, Ray mows down our costs and head count. We see profits improve. But because the roots remain, the expenses and staffing grow back causing our profits to turn into losses."

"That's a good analogy, but what's at the root of our overhead costs?" asked John.

"John, if I knew, I'd have your job," Mark shot back.

Everyone laughed and nodded. Ray could tell they understood that getting the information needed was not going to be easy. It at least made the attacks feel less personal.

John looked at his watch again and stood up. "I think we've had enough for one day. And I think we've accomplished something by airing some of our problems. Our next step is to define three things we can do together to make our accounting system a ten."

No one spoke. John went on. "Let's all prepare two lists over the weekend. First, I want you to brainstorm and write down as many ideas as you can to improve the accounting system. On the other list, I'd like to see your recommendations for things that we could do this month to get our profits back on track. As Mark said, freezing spending is not a sustainable solution to improving profits. We need new ideas. We'll meet here again Monday afternoon at 3:00. All clear? If no questions, have a great weekend."

As Ray followed the rest of the group out of the room, John called him back. *Oh, God,* thought Ray, apprehensively. Maybe John was going to ask for his resignation.

John closed the door before speaking. "Ray, I know you must feel pretty beat up right now, but it was important for us to do this. I need to tell you something, but you can't let it leave this room." Ray nodded.

"I got a phone call from headquarters this morning. They told me that if we don't find a way to improve our profits within the next ninety days, we may all be out of a job."

Ray stared. "Maybe there is a way, but I sure don't know what it is or where to start."

"Neither do I, Ray. But we've got to find one. I know that there's got to be a common-sense answer out there somewhere. All we have to do is find it." Ray nodded, but he didn't see much room for optimism.

"So, see you Monday. And say hello to Gloria and the kids for me." John headed out the door, leaving Ray to turn out the lights and close the door behind him.

Right, Ray thought: *Hi, Gloria. Hi, kids! Guess what? Daddy might be out of a job soon! And how was your day?* He made his way back to his office to get his briefcase and the keys, then walked out to the parking lot. He could feel the tension mounting the whole way, first in his neck and then as it built into a pounding behind his eyes. Turning on his car's ignition, he realized that with all his years of training, experience, and brain power, he didn't have a clue what to do.

3

Ray felt completely alone despite the activity at home. His ten-year-old daughter, Lindsey, wanted to show him a lion she had drawn, and David, who was two years younger, wanted to play basketball. Gloria was asking him about his day, and even the dog wanted his attention as he brought a ball and waited for Ray to throw it. But Ray felt like he was standing alone in the middle of an empty football stadium with no coach to tell him what to do, no team to play with, and no one to cheer. He smiled mechanically at Lindsey's drawing, told David they'd play after dinner, threw the ball once for the dog, and told Gloria everything was fine.

Gloria picked up immediately on Ray's mood. You don't live with someone for twenty years without knowing when something is wrong. She wanted to help, but Ray clearly didn't want to talk about it.

At dinner, she tried valiantly to keep the conversation going. Gloria asked the kids about what happened in school. And then she asked Ray about people she knew at his office in an attempt to draw him out. But Ray, clearly preoccupied, gave only one-word answers to her questions. Although he knew he was making everyone uneasy, he just didn't have the energy to try to make them happy right now.

As she did every Friday night during dessert, Gloria pulled out the calendar to go over the coming events of the weekend. They had started doing this a few years ago when the kids had begun playing soccer. It really did help to know who was going where and who needed to drive on Saturday and Sunday.

Ray interrupted her scheduling. "I have to work some this weekend."

"C'mon, Dad," said Lindsey. "Give yourself a break."

Ray always found it hard to resist his little girl. He knew she had him wrapped around her finger. But he said, "No, really. I have to concentrate on some stuff that's going on at the office." It was hard for him to mask his irritation.

Gloria sighed. "Okay, I'll take the kids to their games on Saturday morning, and then we'll go do something in the afternoon."

Before they went to sleep that night, Gloria tried again to get Ray to talk, but he rebuffed her, saying he was too tired to explain, too tired of everything. After Gloria had gone to sleep, Ray lay awake, replaying the events of the day, things said at the meeting, the things he should have said. Then he remembered his promise to shoot hoops with David after dinner. David hadn't bothered to ask again. Ray chalked up one more failure for the day.

Ray had the house to himself Saturday morning. When they designed the house, Gloria had insisted on cathedral ceilings and lots of big windows. Today the sunshine streamed in through them. Gloria had taken the kids to the soccer fields early, but she had left a fresh pot of coffee for him. She had also left the paper on the kitchen counter. In it were circled ads and articles about things she thought might interest him. Ray enjoyed finding her notes. This time she had circled three things of interest, and next to each one she had put a little question mark, suggestions awaiting his approval. Ray smiled as he looked them over: a harvest crafts fair to be held Sunday, a "multifamily" garage sale, and an ad for a church. The church ad announced a sermon series called "Transforming Principles for Tired Lives." Ray remembered what he had said to Gloria in bed the night before and was touched that she had listened.

Ray stewed over John Brady's assignment all afternoon and busily rearranged numbers and charts, but he made no progress identifying how to improve profitability. He wrote down a few thoughts on costs that could be cut, but they all involved letting people go, which only depressed him. He had canceled his weekly golf game with Bill, a friend, who kidded him about being afraid to lose. Now he wished he had gone. The afternoon wouldn't have seemed such a waste. He still had nothing to offer to John Brady.

"So did you see the paper I left?" asked Gloria when she and the kids returned.

"Yeah, that was nice," said Ray. "I wish I could go with you to the harvest fair tomorrow, but I've still got a ton of work to do."

"Well, what about that lecture for tired people," Gloria asked with a smile. "It might help you, and at least we could be there together."

Ray shrugged. He had his doubts. He and Gloria were not churchgoers. His parents had taken him to Sunday School when he was a kid, but they stopped going when he started junior high. He didn't have anything against religion; it just didn't seem relevant. Besides, they were so busy there really wasn't any time for extra activities like church.

"C'mon," pleaded Gloria, "this guy Reverend Owens is supposed to be a good speaker. Some of the moms at the kids' school have told me about him. I'd actually like to hear him myself. We don't have to join or anything. Why don't we just go listen?"

Ray rolled his eyes. "I guess being too tired won't work as an excuse for this one. So, if you really want to, we'll go."

Sunday was a spectacular October day. There was a nip in the air, the trees were just days away from their full blaze of color, and the sky was clear and the sun bright. Ray could have used the time at home, but he had to admit it was good to be up and around on a morning like this. Gloria had stopped trying to draw him out and was focusing on getting everyone into the minivan on time.

As they pulled into the entrance of Calvary Bible Church, Ray let out a low whistle. The parking lot resembled the one at the mall. There was actually someone directing traffic. The church building and surrounding grounds were impressive. Late-blooming flowers surrounded it and a soaring steeple marked the sanctuary. Most of the people actually looked glad to be there and not like they were just doing a weekly duty. This was all a far cry from the little church Ray had attended with his family as a kid.

At the door, a well-dressed gentleman greeted them with a cheerful "Good morning!" and gave them a program. Gloria and the kids made their way to an empty pew. Ray slid in beside her and sat down.

Ray looked around. The auditorium was new and spacious, with open-beam construction that made the space feel a little like the inside of a huge barn. Instead of stained glass the windows were clear, providing a view of the surrounding countryside and giving a warm brightness to the room.

Ray opened the program and read: "Ten Transforming Principles for Tired People." Ray had to admit, it was a catchy title. *Who isn't tired these days?* he thought. He realized that, subconsciously, he was dreading a boring message about sin. Isn't that what they talked about in church? He'd heard enough about what he was doing wrong at work. He wasn't up to hearing about sin on the weekend, but he could relate to being tired.

Suddenly an orchestra began to play. This was a special treat for Ray, as he missed the days "before kids" when they had season tickets to the Philharmonic. The music was beautiful, just what he needed. Then there was singing, and Ray surprised himself by remembering the words to some of the songs.

During the prayers, Ray's mind wandered, but then Rev. Owens stepped up to the pulpit. He was younger than Ray expected, in his late forties maybe, a little gray around the temples, but fit and tan. Ray wondered if he played golf and was curious about what this man had to say about being tired.

The preacher looked out into the sea of faces and began. "This morning we begin a new series called Ten Transforming Principles for Tired People. I want to preach this series because I'm convinced there are many people in our world who've tried all the fads and formulas the world has to offer. They've tried the theories of well-meaning but misinformed social scientists who claim to have the answers but actually leave people with more questions than they had before. I believe people are tired of the frustrations and stress that overwhelm their lives. I believe people are looking for something worth believing in ... something to help them *enjoy* life, not just *endure* it."

Ray nodded in spite of himself. He was frustrated at home and at work, and he wasn't enjoying either the way he thought he should.

"Unless I miss my guess, there's someone here today who feels overwhelmed by everyday life. Maybe there's been a family crisis and you've lost someone dear to you. Or maybe you're a busy mom and your aging mother needs you to care for her. Maybe things aren't going well at the office and you're worried about your job. Maybe you could use some encouragement in your marriage. Maybe you can't even identify a problem, but you just know you're sick and tired of being sick and tired.

"Well, folks, I believe this series can change all of our lives if we'll open our hearts to what the Bible has to say. We're going to look at ten principles over the coming ten weeks: principles that will work in our lives, principles that will work in our homes, principles that will work in our businesses." Ray was still listening, though the pastor's words reminded him that he needed to get back to his own business problem. Yet he was intrigued and wondered where the pastor was going with all of this.

"These principles," the pastor continued, "will work for anyone, anywhere, at any time, because they are the timeless truths of the eternal Word of God. Each of them will be illustrated for us through the lives and actions of some of the Bible's greatest characters. Some of these people you'll remember from stories you heard as a kid, others you may be meeting for the first time. But all of them can change your life, if you keep an open heart and an open mind."

Okay, okay, thought Ray. *So what are these principles anyway?* He wasn't sure if he could buy into the "eternal Word of God." He wasn't even sure there was a God. But "timeless truths" struck a chord. They must have some merit if they'd proven true through the ages.

As if in answer to Ray's thoughts, Rev. Owens went on. "The first principle is this: *Manage the work before you manage the workers.* Please turn with me to Exodus, chapter 18, where we meet Moses, one of the greatest leaders in all the Bible. Nearly everyone has some idea who Moses was. Some of you imagine him as a baby who was floated down the Nile in a basket and then found by Pharaoh's daughter." Ray recalled making a bulrush basket in Sunday School as a kid. They'd put a doll in it and floated it in the sink. But it occurred to him that his own kids had probably never even heard of Moses, at least not in a church setting.

"Others will remember Moses telling Pharaoh to let his people go, then leading the Israelites out of Egypt and through the miraculously parted Red Sea. Moses was the Hebrew people's leader in the desert when God provided manna to sustain them. And later on, it was Moses who brought down the Ten Commandments from Mount Sinai."

Rev. Owens went on. "I could preach a whole series on the lessons we can learn from Moses' life. His is a life rich in principles. But today I want to focus on a lesson Moses learned from his father-in-law of all people! Exodus 18 tells us this story, which occurred after the manna appeared but before the Ten Commandments were handed down.

"Moses' father-in-law is a priest named Jethro, and he comes to visit Moses in the desert. When he hears about all that God has done for the Israelites through Moses—the escape from Pharaoh, the Red Sea, the manna, the victories over other enemies, the whole works—he praises God for all He has done. The next day, Moses sets about his daily duties while Jethro looks on. I'm not sure I'd want my father-in-law, or especially my mother-in-law, watching me do my job, but I guess Moses dealt with it in his own way." It wasn't until everyone laughed at this that Ray realized that there were over a thousand other people there in the church.

"Anyway," the pastor went on, "most of Moses' day is taken up by settling disputes among the people. As verse 13 says, '. . . Moses took his seat to serve as judge for the people, and they stood around him from morning till evening.' Jethro sees this and asks, 'What is this you are doing for the people? Why do you alone sit as judge while all these people stand around you from morning until evening?' Moses tells Jethro he has all these disputes to settle, and in reply Jethro tells Moses he's doing too much, that he can't do it all himself. Instead Jethro advises him to focus on being the liaison between the people and God as this is his most vital work. He should share the other work that has to be done with men he can count on. So Moses chooses capable men to be leaders and serve as judges. This was the beginning of the system of judges in Israel.

"Now, folks, pay attention here. Jethro was not advising Moses to simply delegate. He was urging Moses to focus on the work he was meant to do. In Moses' case, he was supposed to be the people's representative before God, and he also needed to teach them how God wanted them to live. Trying to resolve every little dispute would have quickly worn Moses out and kept him from fulfilling his mission in life.

"Now, let's think about this. What work are you meant to do? If you're a mom, are you spending more time chauffeuring your kids around than you are leading them into the twenty-first century? If you're a teacher, are you spending more energy on teaching your students what to learn than how to learn? If you're a parent, are you spending too much time focusing on family expenses instead of the experiences that consume those expenditures? Or if you're in business, do you spend too much time managing workers instead of the work? Whatever you're involved in, Jethro's advice suggests that we need to focus on the really important work in life and how best to accomplish it. Moses responded to Jethro's advice in a way that is unexpected. He listened, learned, and responded in a positive way. And, based on what Moses accomplished in the rest of his life, it was good advice."

Ray grabbed a note card and pencil from the back of the pew in front of him and wrote as fast as he could. He didn't want to forget those words: "Manage the work, not the worker." Ray didn't hear much more of what the pastor had to say. He was too busy thinking about how this principle might help him respond to the challenge at work.

4

On Monday morning Ray pulled into his parking space just as Kathi Edwards, his cost accounting manager, was locking her car. Kathi's new red VW Bug suited her bright and unfailingly optimistic personality well. "Hey, Ray, how was your weekend?" Her husky voice always reminded him of Debra Winger.

"Well, it ended a lot better than it started."

"How so?" Kathi asked as they walked toward the building. Ray buttoned his jacket. It was getting chilly in the mornings.

"I'll tell you in a few minutes. Why don't you get settled, grab a cup of coffee, and come into my office. We have to get ready for a profit-improvement meeting with John at three." Ray laid his briefcase next to the picture of Gloria and the kids that rested on the credenza behind his desk. As he snapped open the briefcase, he saw the note card from yesterday's church service resting on top of his work papers. Ray picked it up and read it to himself once again, *Manage the work, not the worker.*

When Kathi came in with her coffee, she caught Ray looking at the card and said, "So what are you reading that's so interesting this early in the morning?"

"I'm not entirely sure," said Ray.

Kathi looked puzzled as Ray said, "I'm going to need your help all morning, so cancel any meetings you have." Ray then transferred the papers in his briefcase to his desk.

"No problem," said Kathi. "My schedule's pretty clear today."

"Good. I know you're aware that our division is missing its profit plan. Apparently, headquarters is upset. I got caught totally off guard by John and the others at the financial review meeting on Friday. I knew we had some problems to address, but I was blindsided by what happened." Ray walked to the greaseboard on his office wall. At the top of the board he wrote the phrase *Manage the work, not the worker.*

Kathi looked blankly at the words and looking a little nervous asked, "Well, what happened at the meeting? Was there some problem with the numbers we gave you?"

"Well, they were wrong, but not in the way you're thinking. To quote John, 'our accounting reports are precisely useless.'" Kathi frowned, puzzled.

"I don't have time to go into details now. John needs two things by this afternoon. First, he wants several ideas for cost improvement that can help us meet the profit plan. Second, we have to come up with some ideas to improve the accounting system. You know, ways to make the data more useful to managers."

"And we have to do all of this in time for this afternoon's meeting?" Kathi said as she wrote the two objectives on her yellow pad. "You're kidding, right?"

"No, I'm not joking," said Ray. "This is serious stuff. I don't want a lot of questions from the staff or any other interruptions, so let's work here in my office today."

Kathi grinned. "That's fine. But to get finished by three o'clock, we're going to need a lot more people in this office than you and me! Shall we bring in some bleachers?"

"No bleachers. You're right. We will need some help. Before we start, do me a favor and call Noel Edwards in the receiving department. Ask him if he can come up here right now for about an hour."

As Kathi began to leave, she turned around with another question. "I almost forgot. Why did you write 'Manage the work, not the worker' on your board?"

"I'll tell you when you get back from calling Noel," Ray replied.

As Kathi went to her cubicle to call Noel, Ray pulled out a copy of the receiving department's actual spending for the first six months. He also got out the notepad on which he had scribbled some thoughts Sunday afternoon. *I hope to God this works,* he said to himself.

The phone rang. It was John. "Hi, Ray. How are things coming for this afternoon's meeting?"

"Well, we're not ready just yet, but we will be."

"Good. I can't stress enough how important it is for us to come up with a plan we can implement right away, and one with immediate results. Headquarters called again just to make sure I understood they mean business."

Stress is right, thought Ray. *Though that's all I need right now—more pressure.* Aloud, he said, "We'll come up with something. In fact, we're working on it right now in my office."

"Do you have a recommendation?"

"I'm just not ready to say yet," Ray said, "but I'm hopeful. I'll see you at three."

As Ray hung up, Kathi and Noel came in. Noel and Ray knew each other well. They had started at Megna on the same day. They had met in the Human Resources office as they both filled out their forms. Since then, Ray had quickly climbed up the managerial ladder, from an entry-level cost accountant position to his present position of division controller.

Noel had done well, too. He had begun as a warehouse material handler and was now the supervisor of the receiving department. Since he spent most of his day on the warehouse floor, he wore blue jeans to work. He loved to give Ray a hard time about having to wear a suit. Ray, on the other hand, always kidded Noel about his now graying ponytail. Both were extremely good at what they did, and over the years, they had helped each other out whenever the need arose.

"Noel, I need to pick your brain."

"What's up?" asked Noel as he sat down.

"Well, there's something new I need to try out, and I think you're the best person to help." Ray handed Noel a copy of the receiving department's expense report, which added up to $780,000. "I'm looking for an answer to a business problem."

Noel grinned. "You've come to the right place if you want to talk business, except I spell it b-u-s-y-n-e-s-s."

"Yeah, well, funny thing, wise guy, because 'busyness' is exactly what I want to talk about," Ray shot back. "I'm working on a theory that perhaps we've been measuring and managing the wrong things."

Noel smiled slyly and said, "Whoa! What made you finally wake up and smell the café latté?"

Ray cracked a small grin. "All I can say is that it was a very recent wake-up call. But the point is, can you help me out?"

"I'll try. But I'm no accountant. What do you want me to do?"

Ray had already started drawing a grid on the greaseboard beneath the words *Manage the work, not the worker*. He labeled the rows in the matrix with each of the costs listed in the expense report for the receiving department. Next to each cost, Ray wrote the dollar amount. Then, double-checking his work, Ray confirmed that all $780,000 was accounted for on the board. As Noel and Kathi sipped coffee and watched, they couldn't figure out where he was headed with all this.

Kathi broke the silence. "I see that the rows are the resources consumed by receiving. What are the columns going to be?"

"Good question. That's the main reason I've asked Noel to join us. Noel, what work do you and your employees do back there in the receiving area?"

"Oh, we do a lot of work," said Noel. "We're busy."

"I know you're busy, Noel. But doing what? You have a terrific team of employees, and I know all of you work hard." Ray paused as he searched for the right words. "But what are the things, the activities, you all spend your days doing?" Ray, pen in hand, looked at Noel hopefully.

"Well, let me see. We receive material and we . . ."

"Hold on," said Ray as he wrote *Receive Material* in bold letters at the top of the first column of the matrix. "Okay. Go on, what else consumes a lot of time?"

"Let me think for a minute. Well, we have to move the material. We either move it to the quality department for inspection or we move it directly to the warehouse."

Ray wrote *Move Material* in the second column. Kathi then asked, "Noel, don't you have to expedite a lot of the material directly to the factory floor? Like parts they urgently need to complete a customer order?"

Noel nodded, but before he could say a word, Kathi continued her thoughts, "It seems like we waste lots of time in accounts payable searching for missing receiving forms. We get the purchase order from Mark's group and we get the invoice from the supplier, but we don't always get a receiving notice from your department."

"Yeah, that's right," Noel acknowledged. "We do waste time making phone calls and waiting for back-ordered parts. In fact, I've got two full-time people assigned to expediting. We try to get the paperwork up here to the office, Kathi, but sometimes we forget. I'm sorry, but our primary job is to help keep the production line running. We can only try to do better."

"We'd appreciate it. I know you're busy, but so are we."

Ray wrote *Expedite Material* at the top of the third column. "Well, what else, Noel? Is there any other work that takes up a lot of your time?"

Noel thought for a couple of seconds. "I think that's about it. Sometimes a couple of foremen and I spend time in meetings, like this one. And there's a pile of paperwork we have to do each week. You know, timecards, reports, and the like."

Ray wrote *Manage Employees* in the fourth column. "Kathi, I need your help. Grab that calculator on my desk. Let's allocate Noel's expenses to these four activities we've written down. Noel, you spent $100,000 on supplies during the first six months of this year. Were any of them used to receive material?"

"Yeah, but I can't be real precise unless you let me go back through all the expense records."

"We don't have time, Noel. We need your best guess right now. I've got a three o'clock deadline for this little experiment."

"Well, let's see," Noel said as he stared at the greaseboard. "I'd say we use about sixty percent of the supplies for receiving, about ten percent for material movement request cards, and the rest for expedite forms."

Ray wrote $60,000, $10,000 and $30,000 on the first row of the spreadsheet under the corresponding activities. "How about depreciation? There was $80,000 of equipment depreciation during the first six months."

"You've got me," Noel said. "I have no idea what makes up that $80,000."

Kathi left quickly and came back with the fixed-asset report. She flipped through the pages until she found the section for the receiving department. "From this, it looks like most of the depreciation is for the eight forklifts you bought a couple of years ago."

"Well, if that's what we're talking about," Noel continued, "I use one forklift for unloading supplier trucks, six for moving material, and one for expediting."

Using these rough ratios, Ray divided the $80,000 depreciation cost and assigned an appropriate amount to each of the three activities mentioned. "What about the overtime expenses?" Ray asked. "Which activities require overtime, Noel?"

"That's easy. We wouldn't have any overtime if it weren't for expediting." As a result, Ray put all the overtime costs in the expediting column.

Kathi jumped into the discussion. "How are we going to allocate the wage and fringe costs, Ray? Don't we need to get the industrial engineers to do a time-and-motion study?"

"We could, but I don't think we need to. Noel, what percentage of your staff's time, including your own, is spent on each activity? Just give me your best guess."

Noel thought a moment. "I'd say we spend about thirty percent on receiving, about the same on moving material, and about fifteen percent for expedites. What does that add up to?"

"That's seventy-five percent," Kathi announced. "Maybe the balance of twenty-five percent goes to managing employees? Does that sound about right, Noel?"

"Yeah. That's good enough for me. Can I go now?" asked Noel.

"Not quite. Just a couple more numbers to go. This is a big help," said Ray as he looked at the board. "Space costs were $100,000."

"What's that?" asked Noel.

"The cost of the floor space in the receiving department. It includes your share of the cost of the building, property taxes, housekeeping, and utilities," said Kathi. "What percentage of the space is used to receive material?"

"About thirty percent," said Noel. "In fact, the percentages are about the same as the ones I gave you for people costs."

Kathi calculated the numbers that resulted and then called them out to Ray so he could write them on the board. "How about all the other miscellaneous expenses? How do you want me to spread them to the activities?"

"Do whatever you want," said Noel, grinning, as he looked at his watch. He'd been there for forty-five minutes. "I need to get back to help the guys. We've got a big shipment of corrugated due in this morning."

"I know you're in a hurry, Noel, but these estimates need to be your numbers, not mine. So what do you think?"

"Well, just use the time percentages. You know, thirty percent for receiving, and so on." Noel started to get up.

Kathi had been adding up the columns as Noel finished. "Ray, the totals are Receive Material–$235,000; Move Material–$235,000; Expedite Material–$172,500; and Manage Employees–$137,500." As he wrote the numbers at the bottom of the spreadsheet, Ray stepped back to look at the board.

"Manage the Work, Not the Worker"
Activity Accounting Report

Receiving Department		Receive Material	Move Material	Expedite Material	Manage Employees
Supplies	$100,000 →	$60,000	$10,000	$30,000	—
Depreciation	80,000 →	10,000	60,000	10,000	—
Overtime	50,000 →	—	—	50,000	—
Salaries	400,000 →	120,000	120,000	60,000	100,000
Space	100,000 →	30,000	30,000	15,000	25,000
All Other	50,000 →	15,000	15,000	7,500	12,500
Total	$780,000	$235,000	$235,000	$172,500	$137,500

Ray mumbled to himself, "Precisely useless versus approximately relevant." The numbers weren't precise, as they were in his traditional monthly accounting reports, but according to John, the old report was useless. The numbers on the greaseboard were only approximate, yet Ray could tell already they were more relevant.

"So does that take care of it? Can I go?" Noel asked as he walked toward the door.

"Yeah," said Ray as he stared at the board. "Thanks. Thanks a lot, Noel. I really appreciate your help. I may be giving you a call later on, but that's all for now."

Ray sat down in his chair. "Kathi, I think we may be on to something useful here. We've always focused on managing head count and spending by department. Maybe instead we should be managing the activities that consume those resources."

Ray looked at his watch. It was already ten o'clock. "Kathi, there's not much time left to prepare for this afternoon's meeting. I want you to prepare three overheads for me. On the first one, list Noel's $780,000 spending by expense type. On the second chart, list the four activities and the total cost of each. On the third, we'll put the spreadsheet we just created on my board."

Kathi looked puzzled. "I'm not sure I understand, Ray. Just an hour ago you said we needed to come up with ideas for cost reduction and accounting system improvement. Now all you want are these three overheads."

Ray grinned and said, "I think we may have accomplished both objectives with this one simple spreadsheet."

"Are you sure?" Kathi said with concern.

"No, to be honest, Kathi, I'm not." Ray walked to his window. "But there's one thing I am sure of. John and his staff aren't happy with the numbers we've been giving them. So what do we have to lose?"

"Our jobs maybe?" Kathi said, looking distinctly less excited about their project and rather concerned about what might lay ahead. "What if this matrix we came up with this morning doesn't fly with the management team? We could be out of a job. Are you sure we're doing the right thing?"

"No, but I just get the feeling that it might be a better way of managing our costs. We'll know more this afternoon if we're right." As Kathi left his office, Ray closed the door and sat down. He picked up the card from church and read once again *Manage the work, not the worker.* He felt good about the spreadsheet they had created. Given Noel's numbers, the principle made sense. Focus on the work, the activities, not just the cost of the workers, supplies, and other expenses. So far so good. But Ray felt uneasy. It just seemed strange that an answer to an important business issue could come from a sermon he'd heard at church yesterday, let alone a story from the Bible.

Ray spent the rest of the morning answering phone calls and questions. Once Kathi gave him the three overheads at about 2:00 p.m., he made some notes and wrote an agenda for the meeting.

By three that afternoon, John and all of his staff had arrived for the meeting, taking the same seats they had occupied on Friday. As John sat down at the head of the table, he said, "Last Friday we agreed to give serious thought to two issues over the weekend: improving our accounting system and improving profitability. Ray, I know you've been working on an idea. Which issue does it address, and are you ready to share it with us?"

Ray plunged in. "Actually, John, I think that I may have found a single solution for both."

"Great. I hope you're right, Ray." John said enthusiastically as he looked around the table. "I'm all ears."

"First of all," said Ray, "I'm going to need everyone's help. John, I'd like you, Mary, Vince, and Chuck to pull your chairs to the left side of the room. And the rest of you, Mark, Chris, Dave, and Dick, pull your chairs over here to the right." As everyone moved to their appointed positions, Ray handed each group a sheet of paper. He gave John's group the traditional accounting report for the receiving department.

Traditional Expense View

Receiving Department	
Supplies	$100,000
Depreciation	80,000
Overtime	50,000
Salaries	400,000
Space	100,000
All Other	50,000
Total	$780,000

To Mark's team he gave the report with the four activities that he, Kathi, and Noel had created that morning.

Activity Accounting Report

Receiving Department		Receive Material	Move Material	Expedite Material	Manage Employees
Supplies	$100,000 →	$60,000	$10,000	$30,000	—
Depreciation	80,000 →	10,000	60,000	10,000	—
Overtime	50,000 →	—	—	50,000	—
Salaries	400,000 →	120,000	120,000	60,000	100,000
Space	100,000 →	30,000	30,000	15,000	25,000
All Other	50,000 →	15,000	15,000	7,500	12,500
Total	$780,000	$235,000	$235,000	$172,500	$137,500

"Okay. I've given each team the June year-to-date spending for Noel Edward's receiving department. Now I'm going to give each group fifteen minutes to identify three ways to cut costs in this department by at least ten percent. When the time's up, each group will present its solutions. Here's a blank transparency and pen to write down your ideas." Ray looked at both groups and asked, "Any questions?"

Chris said, "Ray, I'm a sales guy—in fact, I don't think any of us has ever worked in receiving. How are we supposed to come up with improvement ideas? Even if we could, what would it prove?"

"I know what you're saying, Chris," Ray said, "but I'm just asking for fifteen minutes. It won't hurt you to try. Besides, with a cool tie like that, I'm sure you can do anything." Ray wondered where Chris had found a Superman tie, and the nerve to wear it. The others had already begun talking among themselves, so Chris shrugged and joined them.

The fifteen minutes passed quickly. Ray asked John's team—the one with the traditional accounting report—to go first. Vince Larkin from Quality Control presented his group's ideas. He placed his transparency on the overhead projector and turned on the light. The improvement ideas on the screen were:

1. Eliminate overtime: Save $50,000
2. Lay off one material handler: Save $28,000

Ray asked "Does the other group have any questions for Vince?"

"Yeah," Dick Conway from Engineering said. "Vince, how did you all come up with those ideas? And why do you have only two?"

"Well, first we calculated our goal. Ray told us we had to cut costs by ten percent. So, we looked for cost reductions that would add up to ten percent of the $780,000. Cutting overtime and head count seemed pretty obvious actions to us." Vince looked to his group. "Do we have anything else to add to our presentation?"

"No," Mary said, "I think we did a pretty good job with the data we were given and the time constraint."

As Vince sat back down, Dave Dillon from marketing walked to the projector to present the second team's ideas. "This ought to be good. A marketing guy telling operations where to cut costs!" said Chuck Anderson from Manufacturing. A chuckle rippled around the room, until Dave showed his group's improvement ideas:

1. Eliminate expediting: Save $172,500
2. Reduce "move material" work by 10%: Save $23,500
3. Reduce "manage employees" work by $75,000

"Wait a minute," shouted Chuck. "How do you know Receiving is spending $172,500 on expediting raw materials to the shop floor? Where are you getting your information?"

Ray milked the moment for all it was worth—he loved watching Chuck's reaction—then he put the spreadsheet on the projector.

Activity Accounting Report

Receiving Department		Receive Material	Move Material	Expedite Material	Manage Employees
Supplies	$100,000 →	$60,000	$10,000	$30,000	—
Depreciation	80,000 →	10,000	60,000	10,000	—
Overtime	50,000 →	—	—	50,000	—
Salaries	400,000 →	120,000	120,000	60,000	100,000
Space	100,000 →	30,000	30,000	15,000	25,000
All Other	50,000 →	15,000	15,000	7,500	12,500
Total	$780,000	$235,000	$235,000	$172,500	$137,500

"Here's the secret. John, I gave your team the traditional accounting report for the receiving department, the same type of report you all complained about last Friday. I gave the other team what I'm calling an activity accounting report. Working with Noel, we accounted for his costs by activity. Both reports are based on the same total spending of $780,000. But as Vince showed all of us, the traditional accounting encourages us to eliminate workers. Dave, in contrast, showed us that the activity accounting report encourages us to eliminate work, work that doesn't add value to our products."

Several people started talking, but John raised his voice over the others. "Ray, I think the activity accounting report is pretty easy to understand. In fact, it makes a whole lot of sense. But I'm still skeptical about how this new method can help us reduce costs." While not an overwhelming endorsement, John's words were music to Ray's ears.

"You're right, John. We have a lot more work to do to prove that. But this is an important first step. By my calculations, if we find similar opportunities for cost improvement in every department, we can double our profits this year."

John said, "Maybe activity accounting can address both profit improvement and system improvement. But do you think it can solve all the problems we listed on the flipchart last Friday?"

"Well, this may be a little premature, but I have to say my answer is yes. We can't prove it yet, but I've been thinking through the implications. I believe managing activities instead of costs will answer most of our needs. And I think we could implement this quickly."

Ray flipped to a new page in his notepad, to the one that he had prepared after lunch just in case his experiment went well. "I created the receiving department example this morning with help from Noel Edward. What you saw this afternoon took a little over an hour to create. I asked the questions. Noel provided the answers."

John nodded. "I think it's worth pursuing." As he looked around the table, everyone seemed to agree. "What are our next steps?"

"Well, first, let's expand activity accounting into all the overhead departments as soon as possible. Then, based on what we learn, each department needs to identify profit-improvement opportunities that can be implemented in the next ninety days. If all goes well, we'll be back on track by year-end."

"Does anyone have a better idea?" John asked as he surveyed the faces of everyone at the table. No one responded; they were willing to try Ray's plan.

"Ray, let's get started," John said. "I'm only cautiously optimistic about what will come from your recommendations; nonetheless, none of us has a better idea, so go for it! But we don't have much time. How soon can we review your findings and recommendations? Headquarters is all over my back to give them a plan."

Ray looked at his notes again. "I think I can have the activity accounting information in two weeks. That is, if everyone will go back to their respective departments and explain the importance of what we'll be doing."

Everyone agreed to rally support among their staffs. John stood up, pushed back his chair, and said, "Okay, folks, let's see what we can do. Nice work, Ray."

John and Ray were again the last to leave the meeting room. "Ray, between you and me I have a few questions. First, how much waste do you really think we'll find with your analysis?"

"If the other departments, both shop floor and office floor, are similar to Receiving," said Ray as he looked again at his notes, "I bet we'll find twenty percent waste. For example, twenty percent of our annual overhead budget of twenty million is four million, that's four million in waste."

"Incredible! Even if we achieve a small portion of that, we'll have our profits back in line with objectives. That would be great." John grinned. "But here's the second question: Where did you come up with this idea?"

Ray shook his head slowly. "You wouldn't believe me if I told you. Let's just say it was the last place I ever thought I'd look." Ray walked back to his office, feeling like a new man. The huge weight on his shoulders Friday was now lighter.

He still had to put the plan into action. It was one thing to have the germ of an idea; it was quite another to make it a success. What if he fell flat on his face? It wasn't just his job riding on this; it was John's and the others' too. As Ray walked downstairs, he wondered what next week's principle would be.

5

As he sat next to Gloria in church, for the second time in just seven days, Ray thought about all that had happened over the past week. The last time he had been here, he had felt tired and fed up with his job, just as the preacher had suggested. This morning he was still tired, but he felt much better. It was the kind of tired you get when you've worked hard to accomplish something. Ray couldn't remember the last time he'd had such an energizing, and at the same time exhausting, week. Extending activity accounting into all the overhead departments wasn't exactly difficult, but the tight timetable and the ever-present pressure from headquarters had him and his staff working double time.

Ray was confident they were finally on the right track with this new system, but he was nervous about its long-term impact. He felt a little like a lone cowboy riding an unfamiliar trail. Although he somehow felt he was headed in the right direction, he sure wished there would be some landmarks to point the way. He surprised himself this morning as he realized just how much he had been looking forward to hearing Rev. Owens preach again.

Ray paid more attention as Rev. Owens went to the pulpit. And this time he was ready. He had his pen out and had placed note cards on top of a songbook he'd removed from the pew in front of him.

"We've just begun a new study," Rev. Owens said, "called 'Ten Transforming Principles for Tired People.' This is a ten-week series in which we will look at ten life-changing, life-transforming principles, all of them illustrated through the lives of great Bible characters. We began our study last week by looking at the life of Moses. And the first principle we discovered was this: Manage the work instead of the worker. Moses' father-in-law, Jethro, helped him discover this life-changing principle. I know some of you are still struggling with the idea of learning something from an in-law, but I don't write 'em folks, I just preach 'em." The audience laughed.

"That principle changed Moses' entire life and helped shape his future. It's virtually impossible to imagine what would've happened to Moses if he had not learned the principle: *Manage the work instead of the worker.* Have you tried it yet yourselves?" Ray smiled to himself because he had!

"This morning," Rev. Owens continued, "I want us to look at a second great principle. Get ready to write this down, because this principle can change your life. Listen carefully. *The way to get your needs met is to meet the needs of others.* Now, some of you are probably thinking you're not good enough to meet others' needs; maybe you don't feel like you're quite up to sainthood. And besides, doesn't just meeting your own needs take more time and energy than you have?

"Well, the Bible tells us you don't have to be a saint to serve others. And our character of the day is a perfect example, because today's principle is illustrated by a woman in the Old Testament who was anything but pure. Her name is Rahab."

Rahab? Who's that? Ray wondered as he wrote her name down on the card.

"First, let's get a little background. You might remember how Moses led the Israelites through the desert and all the way to the Jordan River, but he died before they could enter the Promised Land on the other side. Moses had an aide whose son was named Joshua. After Moses died, God called on Joshua to lead his people into the Promised Land. But, as you can imagine, taking possession of the land was no small matter because there were already people living there.

"So before bringing all his people across the river, Joshua decided to check things out, specifically in the fortified city of Jericho. As the story goes in the Book of Joshua, chapter 2, Joshua secretly sent two spies. 'Go, look over the land,' he told them, 'especially Jericho.' So they went and entered the house of a prostitute named Rahab and stayed there."

Prostitute? You've got to be kidding. Ray flushed, hoping Gloria didn't notice. He was remembering an incident that he'd buried deep down long ago. He'd been in Denver on a business trip. Dining alone in the hotel restaurant, he had noticed an attractive woman who also was dining alone.

She was seated at a table in front of him. He pretended not to notice and acted fascinated by his drink. Then they made eye contact.

It was clear she had noticed him, and he felt flattered to have a gorgeous woman pay attention to him. She smiled, he smiled. Okay, so he was flirting with another woman. He knew it was wrong but convinced himself it was harmless since he wasn't really doing anything.

She disappeared when Ray was placing his order, and although he felt relieved, he was also a little disappointed. He knew he should never have looked at her a second time. He'd never do anything to hurt Gloria and the kids, but he had to admit he'd enjoyed it.

Then the woman suddenly reappeared and sat down. She crossed her legs and straightened her skirt, seemingly for his benefit. Gloria was pretty and they were still very much in love, but sometimes he felt like she didn't really appreciate him. Not, at least, in the way the gaze of a beautiful stranger made him feel appreciated.

But the thought of Gloria and his marriage made him get up and ask his waiter to put the meal on his hotel tab. It embarrassed him still to think of the conversation with the waiter.

"Is something wrong, sir?"

"No. I'm just not as hungry as I thought I was."

"Should I have your meal sent to your room?"

"No. Put the amount on my tab."

"Sir?" said the waiter. "Did that woman over there have anything to do with your leaving?"

"Why do you ask?"

"Well, she's been in here several times before, and we've had a few complaints though we haven't been able to prove anything. I just thought, maybe, she had something to do with your leaving so abruptly."

"No. Thanks anyway. Goodnight," he said and went to the elevator. He felt like an idiot. Here he had thought he was inspiring the admiration of a beautiful woman when she was actually just interested in his wallet.

As he entered the elevator, he wondered if the woman really was a prostitute, a high-class, well-dressed call girl. This had never happened to him before, so he didn't know. It didn't matter. The whole experience had shaken him; he never wanted to go through it again. As the elevator stopped at his floor, he decided to call Gloria as soon as he got in his room.

Rev. Owens's voice interrupted Ray's thoughts. "Now, I know some of you are struggling with the idea of learning a life-transforming principle from a prostitute," he said.

"I'll say," Ray muttered under his breath but just loud enough that Gloria heard him.

"What did you say?" she whispered.

"Nothing."

Ray's attention returned to Rev. Owens's message, though he was skeptical.

"One of the reasons I believe the Bible is the Word of God is the way the Bible tells it like it is. It never sugarcoats or covers up our foibles. Instead, the Bible shows how God can take the most unsuspecting, undesirable, unqualified, and undeserving people and use them for His glory. In case you're wondering how God could ever use a prostitute, may I remind you that, if He could use a prostitute, He can use you and He can use me."

Ray knew Rev. Owens was right, but he was still struggling with the whole concept.

"Let's look at Joshua 2. It's one of the most intriguing stories in all the Word of God. The spies are there at Rahab's house. Someone tells the king of Jericho about the spies, so he sends a message to Rahab, telling her to 'bring out the men who came to you and entered your house, because they have come to spy out the whole land.' But instead, Rahab takes the spies up to her roof and hides them under some stalks of flax. When the king's men come to look for them, she sends them on a wild goose chase outside the city gates. She says, 'Yes, the men came to me, but I did not know where they had come from. At dusk, when it was time to close the city gate, the men left. I don't know which way they went. Go after them quickly. You may catch up with them.'

"The remainder of the text tells how Rahab goes up on the roof and talks to the two spies. She tells them how she knew their God had given them the land and how the whole city of Jericho is petrified by the presence of the Israelites. They'd heard about what had happened at the Red Sea and how the Israelites had defeated Sihon and Og, two kings east of the Jordan. She tells them the hearts of the people have melted with fear and she asks them to show kindness to her and her family.

"Well, the two spies tell her that because she had helped them, they will help her. So she helps them escape. Before they leave, the two men tell her to tie a scarlet cord in the window and to keep her whole family in the house with her. Otherwise their blood will be on her hands. She agrees and ties the scarlet cord in the window as they leave.

"Four chapters later, in Joshua, chapter 6, we read about the destruction of the city of Jericho. Many of you are familiar with the story of the trumpets blowing and the walls that came tumbling down. Well, verses 22-23 tell us what happened to Rahab and her family: Joshua said to his two spies, 'Go into the prostitute's house and bring her out and all who belong to her, in accordance with your oath to her.' So the young men went in and brought out Rahab, her father, mother, brothers, and all who belonged to her. They brought out her entire family and put them in a place outside the camp of Israel. By helping the spies, Rahab had secured her family's safety.

"Napoleon Hill, who sold millions of copies of his book, *Think and Grow Rich,* said this: 'The way to get what you want in life is to help enough other people get what they want in life.' Jesus said it this way: 'Do unto others as you would have them do unto you.' It's called the Golden Rule.

"The principle, again, is this: *The way to get your needs met is to meet the needs of others.* Rahab modeled this principle for us by caring for the needs of the two spies. If she had thought only of her own needs, her safety and that of her family, she probably would have been loyal to her king and turned the spies in. But we know now that would have resulted in death for all of them. Instead, by serving God's people, she saved her family, which was something she couldn't have done on her own.

"How many people have you known in life that lived only for themselves and looked out only for their own well being? How many organizations, how many businesses, how many institutions, how many churches, how many people put self-preservation above the needs of others and, in so doing, sign their own death warrant?"

Owens had won Ray's undivided attention. Ray wrote down the words *Meet the needs of others to get your own needs met.* He wasn't sure just how it applied to his own situation at work, but it was worth thinking about. He'd need some time to chew this one over.

In his entire forty-four years, Ray had had two dealings with prostitutes. Both influenced his life: the unnamed stranger in Denver had caused him to take stock of his marriage and family, and now Rahab was about to change forever the way he did business.

6

By ten o'clock Monday morning, Ray had already refereed three battles in his office. Monday was always chaotic, but today won the prize. It started at seven thirty when Mary Forsman from Human Resources and Al Packard, the union steward, arrived unannounced. Rumors had been spreading that Megna Electronics was planning a major layoff. According to Al and Mary, the rumors stemmed from Ray's proposal to extend activity analysis to other departments. They wanted some straight answers.

Ray showed Al the activity accounting report for the receiving department that he had used in the management meeting. It took him just five minutes to explain how activity analysis worked; Al caught on quickly.

Once he had explained the basics, Ray answered the rumors by saying, "If you're asking if management has a plan that involves layoffs, the answer is no. At least not to my knowledge." He paused, then continued. "But is there a reason to be concerned? Possibly, because we're far short of our profit plan. We're having to take a hard look at what we do and how we do it. I think this new accounting approach will help us do that." Ray looked at Al and Mary for their reaction.

Al said, "Well, I understand what you're saying, Ray, but we don't always trust management. Is this activity thing a tool or a weapon? I don't want management to use it like a stick to beat us with."

"Well, Al," said Ray, "it's true that when we're not making enough money, reducing labor expenses is often an easy solution.

It's obviously not good for workers, but it's often not good for the business either. This new approach focuses on how much specific work costs instead of how much the workers cost."

Mary, who had been listening patiently, said, "Al, maybe I can recommend something that we could do to squelch the rumors. Over the years, I've learned that sharing information can go a long way toward addressing employees' concerns and gaining their cooperation. Ray, could you give the workforce a brief overview of your new system, just the way you did here for Al? It's easy to understand once you've explained it, and I think it might really help."

"Sure." said Ray, nodding. "That's a great idea. A brief meeting for all employees might help Kathi Edwards too. The more everyone knows about what we're trying to do, the faster Kathi and her team will be able to gather the departmental activity data. I'll talk to Kathi this morning, run the idea by John for his approval, and then let you know."

"Great," said Mary.

Al nodded, saying, "Fine, but don't assume that by going along with these meetings I'm throwing my support behind this activity accounting thing. I'm still very skeptical about how this information is going to be used."

Not long after Mary and Al left, Chris Meyers burst in. Ray wondered, *What's next?* Just as Chris sat down, Nicole, Ray's secretary, buzzed him on the intercom.

"Ray, Mark Paley from Materials and Vince Larkin from Quality are here to see you."

Ray glanced at Chris before buzzing Nicole back. "Let me see what Chris needs first. Ask Mark and Vince to wait a couple of minutes."

"Okay, Chris," said Ray. "What's up?"

"Well, we've got a problem." Chris tossed a copy of a letter from Megna's number-one customer onto Ray's desk. "Greenbelt Computer says they want a ten percent price reduction next quarter or they're going to walk. I don't think we can afford a price hit like that, but we also can't afford to lose their business altogether. You're our cost expert, what do you think?"

Ray scanned the letter. Greenbelt had two solid reasons for their request. First, Greenbelt faced intense pricing pressure from its competition, so it had to reduce its own raw material costs. Second, Greenbelt had begun to use the Internet and e-commerce to order parts from Megna, so it wanted a share of the savings in procurement costs from reduced paperwork. Ray understood their reasoning, but he didn't have an answer.

"Chris, I honestly can't tell you what to do. I wish I had customer Profit & Loss Statements, because that would help, but I don't. And I don't know what to say about e-commerce savings either. Greenbelt's argument makes sense, but we don't know the cost of the procurement process. I do know purchase prices, but I do not know how much it costs us to supply a product. I wish I could, but I can't help." Ray started to walk Chris to the door. "By the way, nice tie. Black cats, pumpkins . . . subtle."

Chris just grinned and pressed on. "But what about that accounting project John approved last week? Can't you use that to figure out what it costs?"

"I don't know, but it's a thought," Ray said as he opened the door. "Let me think about it. Can you hold Greenbelt off for a while?"

"Maybe for a week or two. I'll just throw them some of that old Meyers' charm." Chris smiled while Nicole and Ray rolled their eyes.

Chris was barely gone before Mark and Vince marched in. *Unbelievable,* thought Ray. *It's like a revolving door.*

"So," said Ray, "what do you all need from the lowly accounting department?"

"Well, as you know, Ray, we're all still looking for ways to reduce costs. We need you to settle an argument. Mark says the favorable purchase-price variance the Accounting Department reports each month is a sign that his purchasing group is doing a good job."

Ray nodded and said, "Right."

Vince continued. "But in the Quality Department we think that zero defects on incoming raw material is the best measure of purchasing performance." Ray nodded his head to that statement too. "Which one of us is right? Is PPV the best measure, or is zero defects? And which measure results in the lowest cost for Megna Electronics?"

Ray was about to say, *"It's a tie,"* until he heard Vince's final question: "Which measure results in the lowest cost?" He stopped and thought for a moment.

"I don't have an answer for you guys. I know that's not what you want to hear right now, but actually you've just asked a question that could help Chris Meyers."

"What does Chris care about raw material costs?" asked Mark.

"Well, our best customer has just asked for a price reduction." Both Vince and Mark shook their heads. "Part of Greenbelt's request is based on the way they do business with us. Without getting into the details, what we have to know before we can give them an answer is how much it costs to do business with them. An answer to the question you guys are arguing about could be the solution. We need to understand the total procurement cost of raw material, not just the purchase price."

"See, Mark, I told you I was right," Vince crowed.

"Hold it, Vince." Ray interrupted. "You're both right. We need to consider the purchase price in addition to all the other costs we incur: the costs of receiving, inspection, warehouse, and so on."

"How can we do that, Ray?" asked Mark. "I mean, this is really important. I've got a dinner riding on the answer. The sooner you prove me right, the sooner old Vince here will have to pay up."

"All I can say at this point, gentlemen, is that I'll add settling your bet to my 'to do' list. Seriously, even though I don't have an answer, it's worth figuring out because it could help me with Chris's problem. I'll see what I can do. Now get out of here and get back to work."

"Right, I've got to create more purchase price variances before lunch," Mark said as they left.

Ray's shoulders slumped as he stood at Nicole's desk. "What a morning. Will you ask Kathi to come in and update me about the activity accounting project?"

While he waited for Kathi to join him, Ray recalled yesterday's sermon about needs. Talk about needs! Every meeting this morning had centered on a different need. Ray looked at his notes from Rev. Owens's sermon. *Meet the needs of others to get your own needs met.* It sounded like common sense, but how could he meet all these needs, and how did they relate to his own needs? On top of cost improvement needs, he had anxious factory workers, demanding customers, and disagreements between departments. And whose need came first?

Kathi entered Ray's office with a huge grin on her face. "What are you so happy about?" asked Ray as he sat down at the small table by the window. He was ready for some good news.

"For one thing, I'm having more fun with this activity accounting project than I've had in ages. Ray, I think this is a stroke of genius."

Ray didn't know how to respond. He was proud of his idea, and, if it was successful, he knew he'd get some recognition. But Ray knew it had all begun with Rev. Owens's sermon. He just smiled and let the compliment pass.

"From the looks of the people coming and going from your office, you've had a busy morning."

Ray said, "Don't get me started."

"Well, read this. It's something I had fun doing this weekend. Maybe it will lighten things up." Kathi laid a sheet of paper on his desk.

Ray picked up the page. It was a memo announcing that "It's Time to Throw Away Cost Accounting's Ten Commandments." Ray laughed delightedly. "Where did you get this?"

"Just read it."

Ray read to himself, nodding and laughing after each item.

COST ACCOUNTING'S TEN COMMANDMENTS

1. Thou shalt close the books every thirty days, whether you need to or not.
2. Thou shalt have only three cost categories: material, labor, and overhead.
3. Thou shalt place absorption of overhead before understanding of overhead.

4. Thou shalt be precise to the right of the decimal point and irrelevant to the left.
5. Thou shalt place direct labor and factory costs before all others when analyzing profitability.
6. Thou shalt place inventory valuation before decision-making.
7. Thou shalt determine praise based on favorable variances to standard cost and budget.
8. Thou shalt expense anything that moves and capitalize anything that sits.
9. Thou shalt assume that where costs are consumed is where costs should be controlled.
10. Thou shalt call nonaccountants "users" of the system, not "customers."

At the bottom of the memo was the request, "Please file in nearest wastebasket."

"Kathi, this is not only funny, it's insightful. I know that you are a person of many talents, but you've outdone yourself with this list. What caused you to write it?"

"Well, based on what you told me about the financial review meeting, it's pretty obvious our department has lost focus. I was just thinking about how our old ways of doing things weren't giving our customers what they needed to do their jobs. You, know, customers like Chris in Sales and Dick in Engineering."

"Anyway," Kathi went on, "I thought it might be a helpful reminder. I can't take credit for the format though. Moses used it first." She laughed.

As Ray scanned Kathi's Ten Commandments again, he said, "Yeah, there's a lot to learn from Moses." He wanted to talk to her about his experience of getting answers about business from the Bible, but then he figured everyone knew about the Ten Commandments. Her list didn't necessarily mean she was using the Bible as a business resource too. Still, he thought it was an interesting coincidence that she had mentioned Moses. But he let it drop and just said instead, "Kathi, this is great. And it did make me feel better. Now, tell me about your progress on data collection for the activity accounting project. Based on the meetings I've had this morning, we may need to speed up the process. I'm getting more questions from our customers, as you call them, than I have answers."

"Well," said Kathi, "the activity interviews are going fine. So far, everyone has been very cooperative. I've taken the liberty of adding one more piece of data to the format you created. I think you'll find it useful." Kathi showed Ray a revised activity accounting report for the receiving department to which she had added Output Measures.

"What are Output Measures?"

"Well, as I was interviewing the other overhead departments to create their activity accounting reports, the issue of workload or 'we're real busy' kept coming up. For example, Mark's purchasing group does an activity called Issue POs (purchase orders). When they talked about how busy they were, I asked them how many POs they'd issued. Then it hit me. We needed to add a workload measure to the activity accounting report. Mark decided to use Number of POs as the workload measure for their activity Issue POs. Mark and his employees defined output measures for each of their activities."

"That makes a lot of sense," said Ray.

"I thought so too. As a result, I've gone back to each department and asked them for output measures. For example, look at the output measures here in Noel's Receiving Department."

Receiving Department		Receive Material	Move Material	Expedite Material	Manage Employees
Supplies	$100,000 →	$60,000	$10,000	$30,000	—
Depreciation	80,000 →	10,000	60,000	10,000	—
Overtime	50,000 →	—	—	50,000	—
Salaries	400,000 →	120,000	120,000	60,000	100,000
Space	100,000 →	30,000	30,000	15,000	25,000
All Other	50,000 →	15,000	15,000	7,500	12,500
Total	$780,000	$235,000	$235,000	$172,500	$137,500
Output Measures		4,000 #of Receipts	1,620 #of Moves	860 #of Expedites	10 #of Employees
Cost per Output		$58	$145	$200	$13,750

Ray looked at the Receiving Department report. "Okay, now I see what you've done. You divided the number of receipts into the total cost of receipts. The cost of the activity becomes the numerator and the workload of the activity becomes the denominator. As a result, you're saying that it costs us $58 each time we receive material."

"Right. But at this point in the project, I don't know whether $58 is good or bad. That's just our cost. But there's another issue I uncovered related to output measures. If we link outputs of each activity to the customers of the output, we can map and measure our processes. I overheard you talking to Vince and Mark earlier about the procurement process. Well, I think activity accounting can help us measure that process plus all the others here at Megna, because it gives us a tool to identify the customer of each activity."

Ray nodded happily. "It makes perfect sense! It seems so simple."

Kathi nodded. "Right, but listen to this. If you take it a couple of steps further, we could even measure the cost, productivity, cycle time, quality, and customer satisfaction of each activity's output. That's way down the road, of course, but logic says it's at least feasible. The point is, we can get information that will truly be helpful to the people who use it."

Ray immediately thought of last Sunday's sermon. Rev. Owens's second principle had been *Meet the needs of others in order to get your own needs met.* Ray thought that, in a business context, it meant "satisfy the customer." He'd been having trouble seeing how it applied, who the customer was in the first place. He realized that Kathi had hit on the answer at two levels. The accounting department's "customers" were the managers of the other Megna departments who used the information he provided; Megna's customers were the companies that purchased products and services from Megna. Activity accounting could meet the needs of both.

Kathi was still talking but he wasn't listening. Instead, he was thinking. It was too weird, both principles had applied. "I wonder what's next?" he mused.

"Ray, are you with me here?" Kathi's voice cut into his musings.

"Yeah, sorry," said Ray. "I was just thinking about all the possibilities. This is good work, Kathi. Keep it up. When will you be finished with the interviews?"

"I'm hoping by next Monday morning," said Kathi.

"Well, let me know when you've finished the activity accounting reports and compiled the findings. We've got to switch from analysis to application real soon. The pressure is on to begin using this new information to make some decisions that will improve profits."

Then, remembering his promise to Al and Mary, Ray changed topics. "I'm going to try to give an overview of our activity approach to Megna's employees. You know, to help them know what we're trying to do and how important it is to the company. It was Mary's idea and I thought it might help you to have the cooperation of all involved. Is that okay with you?"

"Sure, that's great," said Kathi. "But, listen. We keep talking about our system as 'this activity accounting thing.' Shouldn't we call it something so people know what we're talking about?"

"How about just activity accounting? Or, actually, I think of it as activity-based costing. I've actually heard of something by that name, and it's probably close to what we're doing here. Does that work for you?"

"ABC, it sounds simple," said Kathi. "Fine with me." As Ray pushed back from the table and Kathi gathered her papers, Ray heard a familiar knock on the door. It was his best friend Bill, a product manager who reported to Dave Dillon. Ray didn't mind this interruption.

"Ray, my man, how about cutting out early with me today to play nine holes before dark?"

"No way. I'm swamped. I haven't even been able to do one thing I planned to do this morning. Anyway, I already told Gloria I'd be home early tonight to take the kids to play Putt Putt."

"Hmmm. I know I whipped you pretty bad last time. But I had no idea it shattered your confidence to the point that beating the wife and kids at miniature golf is your therapy," said Bill, grinning.

"Get outta here." Ray waved him away. "I'll take care of you next weekend."

After Bill and Kathi left, Ray closed his door to prevent more interruptions. It was just as well that he had so much to do—it might make the week go faster. It wasn't going to be easy to wait for Kathi's findings or Rev. Owens's next principle.

7

With two useful principles under his belt, Ray was determined to collect all ten. Gloria hadn't intended to get the whole family involved in church when she circled the ad for him. In fact, Ray saw his church attendance as work-related. It was something he was doing to improve his job performance, like continuing professional education or a management seminar. It would have been fine with him to let the rest of the family sleep in on Sundays. But Gloria said they didn't see enough of him as it was, and if doing things as a family meant attending church together, then that's what they'd do.

As a result, Ray's children, Lindsey and David, had begun to attend the children's program at Calvary Bible Church. Lindsey had already made friends with another ten-year-old, and David had fit into a group of boys quickly. So far they hadn't complained about going.

And Ray was more upbeat than he had been in a long time; he seemed to have rediscovered a passion for his work. As they walked from the children's wing to the sanctuary, Gloria picked up a visitor's packet from the Welcome Center. After all, if they were going to be there Sundays, they might as well find out a little more about it.

In the pew, Ray held Gloria's hand. He liked being there with her. It was a pleasure that didn't make him feel guilty, unlike many others. Most things that made him feel good were fattening, a waste of time, or shallow in some way. Even when he played golf, much as he loved it, he often felt he really should be working or spending time with his family instead. But sitting there with Gloria, listening to the prelude music, and hoping for some kind of wisdom he could use at work, Ray felt right, though he wasn't sure with what. Himself? The world? God? He just didn't know.

Rev. Owens's opening remarks got his attention. "So far we've seen two life-changing principles: one from the life of Moses and the other from Rahab. The first principle was this: *Manage the work before you manage the workers.* Last week we learned the second principle: *The way to get your needs met is to meet the needs of others.* This morning we'll look at a third principle for improving your life. It may be hard for some of you to swallow, but this principle comes from the life of a teenage boy."

Unbelievable, Ray thought. *We've skipped from Moses to a prostitute and now to a teenager! Owens can sure pick them.* And it was true. The preacher found relevant lessons in the most unexpected places.

"Today," said Rev. Owens, "we're going to look at one of the most famous stories in the Bible, the story of David and Goliath."

Ray remembered the story from when he was a kid. David kills the giant, Goliath, with some stones and a sling. Just remembering how his Sunday School teacher explained the difference between a sling and a slingshot to a bunch of rowdy boys made Ray want to laugh.

The principle seemed obvious to Ray, and, unfortunately, old hat. Themes like *You're going to face big problems in life,* or maybe *The bigger they are the harder they fall,* jumped into his mind. Ray began doubting that this sermon could help him any in his situation at Megna. He knew this story backwards and forwards, and after all, who didn't? The challenge, he thought, was to understand the business application.

Rev. Owens continued. "Most of you have heard this story many times throughout your life. And I know you may be wondering how we can learn anything new from such an old familiar story. Well, today's principle is this: *Focus your energy and efforts on the enemy, and don't waste time fighting with your own friends and family.* This is a tremendous principle that can help marriages, parent-child relationships, work problems, churches, businesses, and virtually every area of our lives.

"The story is found in 1 Samuel 17. The Israelites and Philistines, bitter enemies for generations, have squared off across the valley of Elah. It was a dramatic setting. A streambed, where David gathered his stones, runs through the middle of a mile-wide canyonlike valley with slopes rising about half a mile on either side. The Israelites are encamped on one side of the stream and the Philistines on the other. Can you picture it?

"Now picture this nine-foot tall giant named Goliath who towers over the rest of the Philistine army and advances in front of the Philistine camp. He's wearing bronze armor and has a huge spear. He shouts a challenge across the ravine to the Israelites. In those days, it was common for one man, as representative of his army, to challenge a representative from the opposing army to fight. The winner would secure victory for his army and the losing army would become the winner's subjects. So Goliath challenged any man to represent the Israelite army and fight him.

"The Israelites know they don't have anyone as big as Goliath. Even King Saul, who stands head and shoulders above his fellow Israelites, has chosen to hang back in safety at the rear of his encampment. No one volunteers to fight for Israel.

"But David steps forward. Now David came not to fight but to bring lunch to his brothers. He was the youngest of Jesse's eight sons, and his job was to watch his father's sheep. But Jesse had sent him to deliver the food to his brothers and to return with a report on the fighting.

"When he arrives at the camp, David leaves the food and runs to the front lines to see what's going on. As he joins his brothers, he hears Goliath's challenge. The giant shouts terrible insults and threats. As soon as the soldiers see him, they flee, and this includes David's brothers.

"Now this has been happening for forty days. Goliath taunts the Israelite army twice a day, morning and night, so to the soldiers this is nothing new. But this is the first time David has heard it, and he must have been shocked to see the Israelite army humiliated. Going back to find his brothers among the other soldiers, David overhears talk about what King Saul will do for the man who fights the giant and wins.

"In verse 26 David asks, 'What will be done for the man who

kills this Philistine and removes this disgrace from Israel? Who is this uncircumcised Philistine that he should defy the armies of the living God?' The soldiers say that King Saul has promised great wealth and his daughter's hand in marriage to whoever kills the giant. And, as an added bonus, his father's family will become exempt from taxes! David is listening to all this when his oldest brother, Eliab, shows up.

"Eliab is furious. 'He burned with anger,' the Bible tells us in verse 28, when he hears David speaking with the other soldiers. Eliab lashes out at his little brother with questions and insults. 'What do you think you're doing here, David? Who's watching Dad's sheep? You're a liar! Why are you even here? Who do you think you are?' If you use your imagination, you can almost hear him saying, 'David, isn't that your mother calling for you?'

"David's answer in verse 29 speaks volumes about their relationship. 'Now what have I done?' he asks Eliab, suggesting to us that this wasn't the first time Eliab had belittled David. 'Can't I even speak?'

"Pay attention now because I don't want you to miss what David does. This is the point where you separate the winners from the losers. In fact, this is where you determine success or failure in any endeavor, whether it's in business, relationships, or whatever. It's the turning point, a critical fork in the road where a person must decide which way to go. And the decision will have serious consequences and important implications for the future.

"Let's think about David's choices for a minute. He can accept what Eliab says and go home. Or he can choose to stay right there and fight back, verbally or otherwise, and be justified in doing so. Or he can ignore the real problem, a giant spewing blasphemy and mockery toward the people of God, and instead direct his outrage and energy against his own brother. But what does he do instead? As verse thirty tells us, 'He turned away to someone else and brought up the same matter.'

"What a brilliant move! He turned away! And he persisted in questioning the men about the enemy. Do you see what's happened here? Since we know how the story ends, we know that God had given David a job to do. It would have been so easy for him to become distracted and never accomplish his task. But David resisted the temptation to waste his time and energy in an unproductive, unnecessary squabble with Eliab. Instead, he kept his focus on the important issue at hand and turned away from petty discord.

"David did it and you can too: *Focus your energy and efforts on fighting the enemy; don't waste time fighting with your own friends and family.* How many marriages could have been saved if one mate had simply avoided the temptation to fight and instead focused on the real problems the couple faced? How many promising businesses have failed because they somehow lost focus and got caught up in fighting instead of working together against the competition?

"It happens in churches, too, all the time. Usually it occurs when things are at their best. When you're in the midst of a conflict or facing a severe crisis, it's easy to stay focused. You have no choice. But when everything is cruising along, we often lose focus. And when a church, a business, or a marriage forgets who its enemies are and starts looking for them internally, it's headed for disaster. That's why we need to follow David's example. He refused to get sidetracked. He focused on the goal even when those who were closest to him tried to distract him.

"As we all know, David went on to defeat Goliath, cut off his head, and took his sword, enabling the Israelites to defeat the Philistines. But David's success didn't end there—later he became the greatest king Israel ever had. And that's another sermon. But I can tell you now he started by fighting the enemy, not those closest to him."

Ray thought, *Owens has done it again! Incredible. Those failed businesses he mentioned, Megna's just like them. Employees don't trust the management and the managers are fighting each other. People are so concerned about their own little department that they've turned into a bunch of Eliabs.* Ray remembered the meeting a few weeks earlier when it seemed that everyone was attacking him. The wounds were still tender. He felt a little like David, misunderstood and mistreated, when it hit him. He was just as guilty as the rest.

Ray didn't really care about Megna's success, or rather, he cared about it only in relation to his own success. He winced as he thought about his response at that first turnaround meeting, the anger and defensiveness. And he had to admit that even his efforts to solve Megna's problems were motivated by his own self-image and fears about his job.

Ray thought about last week's principle again, serving others to get your own needs met, and realized that he had failed to apply it to himself. He tended to put his own needs first, but he knew now that if he served Megna's needs, his own needs for job security and respect from his colleagues would be met. And if Megna's success, not his own, became his priority at work, then he was less likely to get caught up in office politics or squabbles with union stewards; he wouldn't be so worried about being right, getting credit, or having to take blame for whatever he did.

In other words, if he could apply the second principle, the third would be easier to do. He realized that he had been thinking of headquarters as the enemy, the one threatening them all with losing their jobs. But headquarters was really on their side; they wanted Megna to succeed. So who was the enemy? What were the forces that threatened Megna with failure? The competition? Sure. Lack of information? Possibly. Ray would need to give it some more thought. For now, it was all he could do to accept personal responsibility for part of Megna's problems. He was another Eliab too.

Although Ray knew the principles made sense, he felt an overwhelming sense of inadequacy. He knew what he was supposed to do now, but he wasn't sure he *could* do it. He understood himself now, more than before, and he had to face up to his weaknesses. Could he realistically change the way he had operated his whole life?

As Rev. Owens was closing the service, Ray quickly wrote down the gist of the third principle: *Fight the enemy, not the people on your side.* He finished just as the pastor led the congregation in prayer. Ray's attention usually drifted during the prayers, but this time the preacher's words were too close to home to ignore. He asked for God's forgiveness when we behave like Eliab, and he asked for the strength we need to be like David. To his surprise, and a little self-consciously, Ray found himself praying alone silently.

8

On Monday morning Ray was in a hurry to get ready for work; he wanted to see what Kathi and her team had learned from their activity accounting interviews. While shaving, he thought about how much was riding on this experiment. If activity accounting didn't reveal some important ways to save costs, they would be back to square one, and they'd have almost no time left to turn the company around. But he also reminded himself that the goal was to make Megna profitable—not to make himself a hero.

When he finished shaving, he looked at his reflection in the mirror. It was the same reflection that always looked back at him. Yet he was a little shaken by what he had learned about himself in church. Having prayed for a change in his motives, he half expected to look different. Maybe it was ridiculous, because he was still Ray, and he knew he looked the way he always had to everyone else. But the experience of admitting that he needed help—and calling on God for that help—made him feel different.

"Earth to Ray!" called Gloria, "You look like you're a thousand miles away. Where's your mind this morning?"

Ray smiled at her. "Already at the office, I guess. I was thinking about work. We have a big meeting today."

Ray ate quickly, grabbed his briefcase and car keys, and then jumped into the car after hugging the kids and kissing Gloria. As he pulled onto the freeway, he noticed the long line of creeping cars and trucks. After no more than a couple of miles, everything came to a complete stop. Slamming on the brakes, Ray groaned and shook his head. *It's Murphy's Law—if you're ever in a hurry, traffic will be stalled,* he said to himself.

Ray tuned the radio to his favorite talk station. A woman was telling a joke. "I went for a hot-air balloon ride this weekend," the caller said, "but we got lost."

"Wow, that's scary," the disk jockey said. "What did you do?"

"Well, the winds blew us over this large open field. Luckily, I spotted a man down below. As we approached him, I yelled, 'Where are we?' He looked up at us and said, 'You're fifty feet over my head.' I looked at my balloon pilot and said, 'Just my luck. That's my accountant down there.' The pilot replied, 'How can you tell?' I said, 'Because what he told me is precisely correct but totally useless.'"

The DJ laughed. Ray smiled to himself but wondered why he had never noticed before how frustrated people were with accountants. He'd heard plenty of lawyer jokes, but few accountant jokes. The fact that the profession had other critics made him feel better. It confirmed that the problems facing his department were not unique to Megna. If people were telling jokes about "precisely useless" accountants, then other companies must also suffer from a lack of useful information. There must be dozens, maybe even hundreds, of companies in the same boat. And he'd thought the phrase was original with John Brady!

The stop-and-go traffic made Ray figure there must be an accident, or a stalled car ahead, but once he reached the five-mile marker, the traffic miraculously cleared up. There was no sign of an accident. *What was that all about?* Ray wondered.

Then, on the opposite side of the freeway, he saw the culprit. A policeman was sitting on a motorcycle and clocking the passing traffic. "What a jerk!" Ray muttered, then thought, *The traffic would be just fine if this guy hadn't decided to sit there during rush hour. Doesn't he know that everyone slows down when they see a policeman, even when they're not speeding in the first place!*

But then Ray suddenly remembered something Chris Meyers had brought up during the financial review meeting. Monthly closings, Chris had said, caused all of Megna Electronics to speed up at the end of each month. But then everything slowed down again once the next month got under way. Chris had called the problem 'Financial Biorhythms,' and the bottleneck in traffic this morning illustrated his point exactly. The monthly sales and expense measurement was just like the cop's radar gun. The accounting department was Megna's "profitability police." Traffic that morning was all smooth and steady until the policeman started trying to catch speeders.

The same thing happens at Megna, Ray exclaimed mentally. *The sale, production, and shipment of product would usually flow pretty smoothly if we didn't have a closing each month. But what if we eliminated monthly closings? It might get rid of some of the unnecessary bottlenecks that keep us from filling orders on time. If we could just come up with some daily measures instead of monthly ones, everyone might be able to focus on satisfying the customer every day. It would be better than the monthly finger-pointing that happens whenever we miss our sales forecast.*

Before Ray could finish his train of thought, he pulled into the parking lot, looking for Kathi's car. She was already there—probably wondering where he was. He jumped out of the car. But eager as he was to get inside, he first laid his briefcase on the hood and opened it. Finding his notepad, he wrote, "Monthly closing = speed check = rubberneckers." It would probably be six o'clock before he had a chance to think about it again, and he wanted to make sure he remembered.

Walking into the accounting department, Ray saw Kathi and her team standing outside his office. It was a good sign and meant that they must be ready to share their findings.

"Where have you been, Ray?" Kathi asked. "We thought you'd be the first person here today."

"I would have been if it hadn't been for the traffic jam on the freeway," Ray said as he unlocked the door. Kathi and the others followed him in: Janis Allen from Personnel, Dick Parsons from Information Systems, Mel Chambers from Industrial Engineering, and Valerie Moon from Quality. Ray knew that Kathi had tried hard to assemble her team from a variety of departments, but seeing the group together made him appreciate her effort even more. Everyone took a seat.

"Well, needless to say, I'm anxious to see what you all have come up with," Ray said as he pulled his desk chair over to the round conference table. "Let's get started."

Kathi handed everyone a copy of the report, which was titled "Activity-Based Costing: Project Findings." Ray's heart was pounding as he opened the report, hoping for the best. "Okay, Kathi. Walk me through this."

"Well, to review, our goal was to define in less than two weeks the cost of all the significant activities performed by every overhead department. In other words, you asked us to analyze every cost below the gross margin line on the P&L. We started out that way. But after a couple of days, it became clear to us that we needed to do the same analysis for the factory. So what we're going to show you this morning is an ABC analysis for the entire company."

Ray looked up. "Great, but how did you get it all done in two weeks?"

"Well, given the time frame, we divided up the work and each of us took different responsibilities. Janis and Mel interviewed each department, like you did with Noel. I discussed cost allocations with each department supervisor during a follow-up meeting. Dick created a spreadsheet model and entered the findings from the interviews into the system. And Valerie followed up with each department manager to confirm the findings before we showed them to you today."

"I'm impressed," said Ray. "Sounds like you had a good plan and a good method. Okay, I can't wait any longer. Let's see what you've got."

Kathi began. "Let's start with Table 1, which shows the current P&L where we're missing the profit plan by $5,300,000. We used actual spending as the basis for our analysis. Table 2 shows an activity-based P&L."

Table 1

Megna Electronics Traditional P&L				
($000s)	Actual	Budget	Variance
Sales	$35,000	$38,000	-$3,000
Cost of Goods Sold	20,000	17,000	3,000
Gross Margin	15,000	21,000	-6,000
	43%	55%	
Sales	4,000	4,100	-100
Marketing	3,000	2,900	100
Finance	2,000	2,200	-200
R & D	4,000	4,500	-500
Personnel	2,000	2,000	0
	$15,000	$15,700	-$700
	43%	41%	
Pre-Tax Profit	$0	$5,300	-$5,300
	0%	14%	

Table 2

Megna Electronics ABC P&L			
($000s)	Value	Non-Value	Total
Sales	$35,000	$0	$35,000
Less: Raw Materials	9,000	1,000	10,000
Less: Procurement Process	2,000	700	2,700
Sales Order Process	2,000	1,500	3,500
Manufacturing Process	6,400	2,900	9,300
New Product Process	1,500	500	2,000
Compliance Process	1,000	500	1,500
Budgeting Process	200	400	600
Maintenance Process	500	500	1,000
Marketing Process	2,000	1,500	3,500
Management Process	390	10	400
People Process	450	50	500
Total Processes	$16,440	$8,560	$25,000
TOTAL COSTS	$25,440	$9,560	$35,000
Pre-Tax Profit	$9,560	-$9,560	$0

Ray looked at the two profit & loss statements side-by-side. At first he was confused. He circled the sales and pretax profit numbers on both. Even though the two reports looked completely different, they both started with $35 million in sales and ended with the same zero profit: "I don't understand what you're showing me. Can you explain it?" he asked.

"I'm going to let Valerie explain it to you, because she's the one who came up with the idea."

Ray looked over at Valerie as she turned on the overhead projector. Valerie was an attractive young Korean woman. Ray didn't know her well. She didn't speak much at meetings, but she had such a reputation for her intelligence and insight that people were always seeking out her opinion. "Ray," she said, "as you know, we've been trying to implement Total Quality Management for the past two years at Megna. It's been slow going because the benefits of improved quality aren't reflected in the financial reports. As a result, John and other senior managers have not been overly supportive of TQM. But I'm pleased to tell you this morning that I think we have found an answer to my TQM needs in activity-based costing."

"That's great, Valerie, but we need to come up with ideas to reduce costs," Ray said.

"I understand that, Ray. But I think we have a method here to do both. We can reduce costs *and* improve quality. Let me try to explain why I'm so excited about this. You see, after I reviewed the activity analysis from the first three interviews that Janis and Mel completed, I offered two recommendations. First, I suggested that we link the activities we found in each department to specific business *processes*."

"What do you mean by processes?" asked Ray.

"Well, most organizations like Megna are managed and organized by department. You know what our organizational chart looks like," said Valerie, "but in reality, Megna's daily operations are accomplished through a series of business processes. To say it in another way, Megna is managed vertically but actually operates horizontally."

"Can you give me an example?" said Ray.

"Okay," said Valerie. "Let's take the receiving department as an example. Noel supervises that department. He has both a head count budget and an expense budget. One of the activities in his department is *Receive Material.* This activity is a step in the *Procurement Process.*"

"Wait a minute, you're losing me. What do you mean by that term 'Procurement Process'?"

Valerie paused for a moment to think of an illustration "Do you ever help your wife with grocery shopping?"

"That's kind of a personal question," Ray said, smiling, "But, yes, I usually go to the store with her on Saturday mornings."

"Well, what's the first thing you do before going to the store?"

"Gloria gets our shopping list."

"And what's the next thing you do?"

"We drive to the store."

"Okay. And then what?" prompted Valerie.

"We get a shopping cart and go through the store picking out the items we have on our list."

"Good, keep going," said Valerie.

Mel smiled and interrupted. "Ray, did you remember to get the Fruit Loops?"

"I take the fifth," said Ray as everyone laughed.

Valerie said, "Go ahead and finish the shopping trip."

"Well, we take the cart to the checkout counter, pay for the groceries, take the sacks to the car, drive home, unload, and put them away."

"Fine. Now, what you've done is describe your family's Procurement Process. We also have a Procurement Process at Megna Electronics. Your first activity was *Create a Purchase List.* The first activity of Megna's procurement process is similar. It's called *Run MRP*—the Materials Resource Planning system. The activity *Receive Material* is one of the activities in Megna's Procurement Process," Valerie continued.

"Is Table 3 the Procurement Process?" interrupted Ray.

"Right," Valerie affirmed. "If you look back at Table 2, we found ten processes in Megna; Procurement was one of the ten."

"Wait a minute," said Ray. "Let's see if I understand this. Every activity in every department was assigned to a business process. Right?"

Table 3

Procurement Process

	Value	Non-Value	Total	Output Quantity	Cost per Output
Run MRP	$805,000	$0	$805,000	100	$8,050.00
Issue P.O.	800,000	0	800,000	16,000	$50.00
Expedite P.O.	0	400,000	400,000	4,000	$100.00
Receive Material	235,000	0	235,000	4,000	$58.75
Inspect Material	0	250,000	250,000	560	$446.42
Certify Supplier	60,000	0	60,000	20	$3,000.00
Pay Invoice	100,000	50,000	150,000	8,000	$18.75
	$2,000,000	$700,000	$2,700,000		
	75%	25%	42,100 parts		
			$64.13 per part		

"Yes," said Kathi. "But the real eye-opener for me was the second thing Valerie recommended."

Ray said, "And that must be the *Value* and *Non-Value* columns on the activity P&L. Am I right?"

"Yes," Valerie explained. "In one department after another, a lot of the activities were caused by errors. For example, in the receiving department, they have to expedite parts—an activity—because of errors made by our vendors or, in some cases, mistakes made by our own purchasing and planning departments. To quantify the costs of errors, I suggested that we classify each activity as *Value* or *Non-Value*."

"What do you mean by *Value* and *Non-Value?*" Ray interrupted.

"*Non-Value* activities represent waste," replied Valerie. "We asked the employees in each department if there were any activities that were the result of mistakes made by another department, a customer, or a supplier. If they answered yes, we labeled those activities in Tables 2 and 3 as NVA, for *Non-Value-Added*. We also asked them which activities they would like to spend less time performing. Those tend to be *Non-Value* activities. Activities that employees enjoy doing tend to be *Value*."

"You mean to tell me our own employees believe that we have $9,560,000 in waste?" said Ray.

"Yes, that's what it says," exclaimed Kathi. "We could have made $9,560,000 this year if we hadn't had any waste!"

"I'm sorry to be a slow learner," Ray said. "Explain to me again how you all converted our traditional P&L into the ABC P&L."

"It was as easy as 1, 2, 3," said Kathi, smiling. "The first step was to interview every department and create an activity accounting spreadsheet. Notice that we added the output measures we discussed last week at the bottom of the spreadsheet. Remember? This was the measure of the workload of each activity. Dividing the output quantity into the activity cost gave us an interesting number."

"Okay, I'm with you. What's next?"

Kathi went on: "The second step was to ask the employees in each department to label their activities as *value* or *non-value*, as Valerie just explained."

"You let *them* classify the activities?" Ray said.

"That's right. We didn't want to serve as the judge and jury of *value*." Kathi replied. "What you see is what they said."

"Wow," Ray said, shaking his head.

"The third step," said Kathi, "was to classify each activity into a business process. Valerie came up with the list of processes from her TQM books, and then Dick figured out a way to program the computer so that we could report activities by *value, non-value* and business process."

"You've outdone yourselves," said Ray. "This is fantastic!" He looked at his watch. "It's almost lunch time, but I have one final question. On the Procurement Process report it looks like you've divided the 42,100 raw material parts we purchased last year into the $2.7 million process cost. Why did you do that?" Ray asked.

"Since we've divided the cost of each activity by an output quantity in the activity accounting spreadsheets, we thought we'd do the same for each process. Therefore, we divided Procurement Process cost by its output, raw material parts. We could potentially use the $64.13 per part for product costing." Kathi explained.

"Give me an example." Ray requested.

"Currently we allocate overhead cost to our products based on direct labor. Our overhead rate is 400%. If a product has ten dollars of direct labor, we allocate forty dollars of overhead. This is a simple method, but it is likely causing us to allocate too much overhead to high-volume, labor-intensive products and undercharge low-volume, low-labor products. Using ABC we can break down overhead into process costs. Then we can allocate processes to our products using process outputs." Kathi pointed back at the Procurement Process report. "For example, if a product has five raw material parts, we would allocate $320.65. If a product has fewer parts, it would get less procurement cost."

Ray responded "That makes so much sense it's scary. ABC is simply organized common sense."

Although everybody smiled, they seemed not to share Ray's enthusiasm. As they walked to the cafeteria, Ray pulled Kathi aside and asked if anything was wrong. "Am I imagining things, or is the team not as excited as I am about this report?" he asked.

"I think we're just a little frustrated," Kathi said, "because we don't know where to go from here. We have some interesting findings, but nothing that will affect our P&L immediately. We're just afraid that if we don't increase profits soon, we may all be out of a job before long."

Ray wondered if John Brady had told Kathi about the word from headquarters, or if everyone could just see the writing on the wall. He said, "Maybe so, but your team has clearly shown that even people from departments with conflicting interests can work together to solve problems. I'm convinced from this morning's meeting, and the report you prepared, that ABC is the smooth stone we need in our sling." Ray smiled, pleased at his analogy, and went on. "It's easy to pick up and it heads straight for the target if you aim it right. If we can just remember we're all on the same side, we may be able to slay a Goliath or two."

"Well, you're sounding very philosophical today. Is there anything else going on that I should know about?" Kathi asked as they approached the cafeteria.

Ray was tempted once again to tell her about the three principles he had learned, but he held back, saying only, "No, nothing."

Then he saw Al Packard from the factory, who said, "Hey, Ray. Is this Friday the end of the month?"

"Yep," said Ray, wondering at first why Al asked, but then he remembered about the traffic that morning. Everybody really did plan their lives at work around the monthly closing. "What a waste of energy!" Ray complained. "Maybe someday I really will get rid of monthly closing."

As Ray pushed his tray down the cafeteria line he thought. *Principle One was to manage the work. We've done that by defining work using activity analysis. Principle Two was to satisfy others' needs.* Non-Value *activities certainly don't effectively meet needs of customers, suppliers, stockholders or employees. In the short term, we must find ways to reduce costs, especially waste.* Value *versus* non-value *analysis can help with that. Principle Three was to attack the enemy, not each other. It looks like ABC is going to give employees from different departments a common language to help them work together in business process teams to achieve common goals. So far so good, but now where do we go?* "I wish I knew what Principle Four was," Ray thought aloud.

"Is it done yet?" Ray felt a tap on his shoulder and turned to see John Brady at his side.

"No," said Ray, "we're not finished. But we've got some exciting information to share with you. Can I bring Kathi's team up after lunch and review it with you?"

"Sure," replied John. "I'll clear the decks."

As Ray paid for lunch, he thought again how nice it would be to know Principle Four before finalizing the next steps.

9

Ray had always been such a workaholic that no one really took him seriously when he said he was taking Friday off to play golf. But sure enough, he didn't come in and had already played nine holes with Bill before anyone realized he probably wouldn't be in at all.

At first Ray had doubted whether he could afford a whole day off. It didn't seem right, given the seriousness of the situation at Megna. But John Brady, impressed with the findings of Kathi's team, had requested that each department develop some steps to cut costs based on the activity analysis. So there really wasn't much Ray could do at this point, and he could use a break.

Bill and Ray sat in the clubhouse overlooking the eighteenth green. It was a gorgeous day. Dozens of huge oak trees surrounded the final hole. The grass was like carpet. Ray and Bill had managed to get a table by one of the large picture windows forming an almost perfect half circle around the green. It was a breathtaking view, and the food lived up to the view. Because Ray and Bill had teed off early, they had beaten the lunch crowd that usually made it almost impossible to get a table at noon.

They took their time and savored the hickory cheeseburgers and Cokes. It was great to get away from the office. Bill and Ray agreed they should do it more often as they reminisced about good times and talked a little business too.

"So," said Bill, "it sounds like you're onto something big with this activity-based costing. Where did you come up with it anyway?"

"Well, I haven't told anyone yet. Promise you won't laugh?" said Ray.

"Hello, Ray. This is your old buddy Bill speaking. Would I laugh?"

"Actually," said Ray, "you might. The truth is, we've been going to church, that big one over by our house. And, well, I've been learning a lot."

"How to be the savior of your company?" Bill asked sarcastically.

"Oh, please," said Ray, rolling his eyes. "That's not the idea. But I have learned some lessons there that can apply to real life. It's not just a bunch of old words and old stories." Bill cocked an eyebrow, and Ray added, "Okay, I know it's hard to believe coming from a first-class pagan like me, anyway," said Ray.

"You can say that again," said Bill.

"I know it's out of character, but it's been an amazing experience for me so far. Three weeks running now, the preacher has explained a principle that has applied directly to what's going on at work. It's uncanny. See, he finds these characters in the Bible, like Moses for example, and—"

"Whatever, Ray," Bill interrupted him, "This is a clubhouse, not a church, so let's not go off the deep end."

"But . . ."

"Enough already. If religion is working for you after all these years, fine. Just spare me the details, all right?"

"Okay, okay. I didn't mean to get your back up. I just haven't felt comfortable talking to anyone else about it, and it's the most amazing thing that's happened to me in a long time."

"Well, all I can say is that it hasn't helped your golf game. You're still down four strokes." Bill grinned as he signed the ticket and added, "Ready to go, reverend?"

They left a generous tip, waved to a few friends at other tables, and grabbed some mints as they headed out. When they got to the cart, Ray's pager was beeping. He reached into his golf bag and looked at the number on the pager's display.

"Who's this?" he wondered. The number wasn't familiar. Only a few people had his pager number: Gloria; his secretary, Nicole;

his attorney; his stockbroker; and Bill. It wasn't any of their numbers. "Hey, do you recognize this number?" Ray asked, showing Bill the display.

"Nope," said Bill. "674-4000. No idea."

Ray noted the last four numbers—it was probably a business number of some kind. "Oh well, let's go," he said. "I'll deal with it later." He tossed the pager into his bag, jumped in the cart, and put his golf glove on his left hand.

It was three o'clock and getting a little chilly when Ray and Bill finally decided to call it a day. Ray thought as he drove down his own street how lucky they were to live in such a beautiful area. The homes were mostly new, and big. Gloria's chrysanthemums were brilliant in the late afternoon sun. When Ray pulled into the driveway, Gloria's car was gone. He parked, checked the mailbox, and went into the house through the garage. Apparently Gloria hadn't gotten around to picking up the family room yet. There were still newspapers lying around, and David had left a #23 Bulls jersey lying on the couch. He was planning to go trick or treating as Michael Jordan for Halloween. Ray gathered up the papers and, enjoying the rare quiet, headed upstairs to take a quick shower.

What a great day. A ten on a scale of one to ten, he thought as he lathered up. The phone rang twice, but he couldn't hear it.

Dry and in fresh clothes, Ray went back downstairs, and this time he noticed the light blinking on the answering machine. Caller ID displayed the same number that had been on his pager; whoever it was had apparently called several times throughout the day. "Who is this?" he muttered. He pushed the button to listen to the messages but only heard the repeated click of a caller hanging up.

There was nothing to do but call back and find out. But just as he was about to dial, the phone rang.

"Hello."

"Ray!" It was Gloria's voice and he knew instantly that something was wrong. She sounded like she had been crying.

"Honey! Where are you? What's wrong?"

"It's Lindsey, Ray! We're at the hospital."

"What happened?"

"Lindsey's been hurt real bad. We need you here now."

"Oh, my God! Where are you?"

"We're at Columbia Medical Center, you know, the one over on Lancaster Boulevard."

"Is David with you?"

"No, he went home with a friend after school. I've called and he's going to sleep over."

"Okay. I'm on my way."

Ray hung up the phone and flew upstairs to grab his keys, wallet, and shoes. Why hadn't he returned the call sooner? He ran to the car and tore off in the direction of the hospital.

He ignored the speedometer and ran at least six red lights. His daughter was hurt, and he didn't even know what had happened though he played out a hundred different scenarios in his mind. As he turned onto Lancaster Boulevard, he saw the hospital in the distance. He pulled in at the main entrance and screeched to a halt under the large canopy. He jumped out, ran through the double doors to the admissions desk, and shouted Lindsey's name.

"Lindsey Miller! Where is she? I'm her father!"

The volunteer tried to pull the name up on the computer, but it wasn't there.

"When did they bring her in, sir?"

"Ma'am, I don't know. She's been in some kind of an accident. I don't know what happened and I don't know where or when it happened. I just need to find her." He fought the urge to scream.

"She's probably in emergency." The volunteer stood up and pointed down the hallway to his left. "Just go down there to the red doors. Turn left and you'll be in the emergency room."

He ran down the hall and burst through the doors into the emergency waiting room. As he scanned the room, he saw Gloria in the far corner with their neighbor, Sandy.

When Gloria saw him, she crumbled and ran to him sobbing, as if she had held it all together just until he got there. "Ray, Lindsey's hurt, bad. And it's my fault, Ray. Oh, my God."

They stood in the middle of the waiting room holding each

other, oblivious to anyone else. Ray led Gloria to a chair in the corner and said, "Honey, tell me what happened." Haltingly, Gloria began to speak.

"Lindsey didn't feel well this morning, so I let her stay home from school. She slept until about nine, then woke up and told me she was feeling better. At about nine thirty, Sandy came over for a cup of coffee. We sat on the front porch while Lindsey played upstairs. Then she came out and asked if she could ride her bike in the driveway. I said it was okay and even helped get her bike out of the garage." Gloria swallowed hard before going on.

"She'd been riding up and down the driveway for just a few minutes when we heard her scream. She'd gotten her shoestring stuck in her pedal and couldn't put the brakes on as she headed down the driveway toward the street. We ran to help, and then we saw the delivery truck coming up the street."

"Oh, my God," Ray said as he covered his face with his hands.

"Honey, I'm so sorry. I couldn't stop her," said Gloria.

"What happened to her, Gloria? Tell me what happened."

"Well, she couldn't stop, and I guess the delivery man didn't see her until it was too late."

"And then what?" Ray was almost shouting. "We live on a cul-de-sac! For God's sake, we built our house on a cul-de-sac! How does my daughter get hit on a cul-de-sac?"

"Ray, I know, I know. It wasn't supposed to happen but it did. It was an accident. And it's my fault. I should've made Lindsey go to school. I shouldn't have let her ride her bike. I just want it to be yesterday again, but as hard as I try, I can't turn back the clock." Gloria was sobbing as Sandy came alongside and put her arm around her.

"It's all right, Gloria," Sandy whispered. "It's all right."

"How bad is it?" he asked.

Sandy looked at Gloria, then at Ray and said, "She's been in surgery for several hours now. The bumper of the delivery truck hit her on the forehead and threw her against a parked car where she hit the back of her head. She's got some very serious head injuries and they're trying to take the pressure off her brain right now. Lindsey was unconscious when we got to her in the street and hasn't been awake since. They told us she's probably got a fractured skull and a severe concussion. It's not good, Ray."

Until now, Ray had felt nothing but fear, cold looming fear that had sped him to the hospital and through the corridors to the emergency room. He sat down now and let the news soak in. Tears of anger, bewilderment, and grief began to well up. His daughter was in pain and danger, and there was nothing he could do for her.

It was already dark when the doctor came into the waiting room and asked for the Miller family. The name "Miller" startled all three of them. "Here," Ray said as he got up and headed toward the doctor. Gloria was right behind him, but Sandy hung back, motioning that she'd wait there.

"I'm Dr. Cochran. Let's go in here, shall we?" the doctor said as he ushered them into a small consultation room off the waiting area. He shut the door and took his glasses off as they sat down.

"How is she?" Ray asked immediately.

"Well, Mr. Miller, the prognosis isn't good. Your daughter has been in a very serious accident and has sustained severe trauma to her head and neck. We believe there may be several fractures in her skull, especially in the back of her head. We've spent the last several hours trying to relieve some of the pressure on her brain. Also, there were numerous lacerations and abrasions on the upper third of her body. We've cleaned those all up; some of them required stitches."

Gloria asked the key question. "Is she going to make it?"

"Well, it's a little too early to tell. The first thirty-six hours after an accident like this are extremely critical. She's in a coma right now and we're not sure if there's been damage to her spinal cord. We immobilized her due to the severe trauma she'd had. I wish I could give you some good news, but all we can do now is wait and see . . . and pray."

His last few words seemed to hang in the silence of the small cubicle. It was almost as if no one was breathing. Ray could hear the ticking of the clock behind the doctor's head.

Breaking the silence, Ray asked, "Can we see her?"

"Yes," said the doctor, "but only for a few minutes. The best thing now is to let her rest and allow the medicine to take effect.

I suggest you all go home and get some rest yourselves. We'll call you if there's any change in her condition."

"I'm not going anywhere!" Gloria protested. "I'm staying right here with my daughter." She started to cry again.

"I understand, Mrs. Miller," said Dr. Cochran. "But there's really nothing more you can do for her right now. She needs rest more than anything." He opened the door to leave and said, "One of the nurses will come and take you to see your daughter."

Ray and Gloria sat speechless. This couldn't be happening to them; they were a picture-perfect family. This only happened to people in magazines, movies, and make-believe. It seemed unreal.

Soon a nurse came to get them, and they followed her numbly into Lindsey's room. Ray stared at his unconscious daughter. She was undeniably real and so were her bandages and the IV at her side. They did what the doctor had suggested and stayed only a few moments before reluctantly leaving the hospital. On the way home, Gloria tried to sound hopeful, saying that Lindsey looked better than she'd imagined. Ray just felt sick.

When they got home, Ray called their parents—he and Gloria took turns talking—and by the time they got off the phone it was late. They were both exhausted and went straight to bed. There was nothing left to say, and they fell asleep quickly, exhausted from the day.

Saturday morning, Ray lay in bed with his eyes closed. It was as if he thought he could postpone the pain by simulating the unconsciousness of sleep. But no matter how hard he tried, Ray couldn't escape two images in his mind: Lindsey unconscious in the hospital, and the doctor in the consulting room, unable to guarantee that she would live.

Ray and Gloria spent all day Saturday in the waiting room outside ICU. This time David was with them. He was sorry Lindsey was hurt, but he was too young to understand the seriousness of it. The hospital bored him; he wanted to go home and play with his Nintendo. Ray's emotions swung from wanting to cling tightly to David, his only other child to wishing he didn't have to deal with him.

As the afternoon wore on, a few close friends and relatives

came by. Bill came late in the day. He didn't know what to say to Ray except, "I'm sorry, man," but Ray was touched that Bill had come. Seeing him made Ray remember how perfect everything had seemed yesterday: a beautiful day on the golf course, good food with a good friend, and a church that was helping him be a hero at work. He hadn't even thought about his healthy family being something special to be glad about yesterday. It had been all about the weather and golf and himself.

Gloria placed Lindsey's Walkman and favorite teddy bear on the windowsill by her bed in the morning. The window looked out onto a lawn and three brilliant yellow oaks. The room itself was yellow, which was something Ray would not have noticed, except that Gloria had tearfully pointed out that it was Lindsey's favorite color. Already some vases bright with flowers had accumulated, the universal gesture of helpless but concerned friends and family.

Ray and Gloria had been allowed to see Lindsey once in the morning for two minutes, again in the afternoon, and once again around dinnertime. There had been no change in her condition all day. David's best friend had invited him to go trick or treating and then sleep over, so Ray took him there and then went home to sleep. Sandy had offered to watch David on Sunday so Ray could be at the hospital while Gloria went home to get some rest.

After Ray and David left for the night, Gloria went to get some coffee. Looking through her purse for some change, she found the visitor's packet from Calvary Bible Church, happy to have something to read while she waited. As she sipped her coffee, she flipped through the pages until she saw a bright yellow sheet. In big letters written across the top of the page it said: "NEED HELP? CALL OUR 24-HOUR PRAYER CHAIN." She didn't exactly know what a prayer chain was, but she remembered the doctor's words, "All we can do is wait and see . . . and pray."

Without thinking further, Gloria got up and called the number on the card. A lady answered and listened patiently to Gloria's story. She promised that the church would pray for Lindsey and the whole Miller family. Gloria sat down, knowing she had done all she could. There was nothing left to do but wait and see, and get some sleep.

10

When Ray arrived at the waiting room Sunday morning, Gloria was gone. In a panic, he went to the nurse's station, fearing the worst. But they had just moved Lindsey during the night to a more private room in ICU so Gloria could stay with her there.

"How is she?" Ray asked as he entered the room.

"No change," said Gloria, who looked exhausted but tried to put up a brave front.

"Has Dr. Cochran been in?"

"Not yet. The nurse said he would probably be in this afternoon. Don't you think her color looks better? And look, Ray, they've cleaned her up some more." She burst into tears.

He put his arm around her and said, "Honey, you're tired. You need to go home and get some rest. Sandy said David could spend all day at their house so you can go home and get some sleep. I brought some work with me, and I'll be fine. You can call me after awhile, okay?"

"Okay," she said, "but call me if anything changes."

After Gloria left, Ray stood and looked at Lindsey for a few moments. She was sleeping peacefully despite all the stitches and bandages. The nurses had brought the flowers from the other room, and more had arrived. This room was yellow, too, with floral curtains. *A regular garden spot,* grumbled Ray cynically, but he was grateful that it didn't seem as cold and depressing as some hospital rooms could be. And all that really mattered was the care Lindsey received.

Ray spread his work out on a little side table and dug in. Work seemed so irrelevant now, but he knew he had to keep at it. At the very least he needed to keep his job for the medical insurance, and the work was a distraction. Pounding on his laptop was more productive than putting his fist through a wall. It occurred to him that he wished he knew what Principle Four was, but there was nothing he could do about it now.

Although Ray thought he'd had a good night's sleep, he soon fell asleep again in the chair. A knock woke him up.

"Excuse me, may I come in?" The male voice startled him.

"Sure, come in," Ray said, yawning and running his fingers through his hair.

"Hi, I'm Rev. Owens from Calvary Bible Church."

"Rev. Owens!" said Ray, extending his hand. "It's nice to meet you. Why are you here? I mean what brings you here?" Ray was embarrassed and searched for something else to say.

Rev. Owens smiled. "I hope I'm not intruding. I understand you've been through a lot in the past few hours."

"How did you know?" asked Ray.

"Someone called our 24-hour prayer chain and asked us to pray for your daughter. When I heard the message, I thought I'd come by this afternoon and pray with you."

"I don't know what to say," said Ray as he blinked back tears.

"Well, why don't we pray over your daughter?" Rev. Owens said comfortingly as he put his arm around Ray. Ray finally broke down. He wept as Rev. Owens prayed for God's comfort and healing. Ray felt ridiculous for his tears, but he figured that preachers had seen a lot of grown men cry.

When Rev. Owens finished praying, Ray got a hold of himself and thanked him for coming.

"Oh, I almost forgot," Rev. Owens added. "I brought this for you; it's a tape of our service this morning. If there's anything else we can do to help, please don't hesitate to call me."

After Rev. Owens left, Ray slumped down in the hospital chair and looked at the tape. He couldn't believe it. Rev. Owens had taken the time to come to the hospital and pray for his daughter, and then had also left him a tape. Ray already knew the message would help him with his work, but how could Rev. Owens have known?

He placed the tape in Lindsey's Walkman and turned it on. He'd forgotten about church this morning, because all that mattered right now was Lindsey. In fact, he wasn't even sure he wanted to go to church after what happened to Lindsey. He was disappointed and even angry at God. *After all,* he thought angrily as he reflected, *look what happened. I went to church. I even prayed my first prayer in years, and look what God let happen. I thought God was supposed to love and help and protect us.* But then Rev. Owens had come and prayed for Lindsey, which had touched him. Ray didn't know what to think at this point. He hit "Play" and the tape started.

"This may be the most important message so far in our new series on life-transforming principles." Rev. Owens sounded the same on tape as he'd sounded just five minutes earlier. "Today we're going to look at the life of one of the Bible's most colorful characters. His name is Jonah. Let's turn to the book that bears his name. You'll find it in the second half of the Old Testament, between Obadiah and Micah."

Ray turned off the tape and fumbled first through the nightstand and then the tray table by Lindsey's bed. *I knew there'd be one here someplace,* he said to himself as he found a Gideon Bible. He couldn't find any of the books Rev. Owens had mentioned, so he looked up Jonah in the table of contents and then found the right page number. He picked up his pen and legal pad and turned the tape player back on.

Rev. Owens brought the story to life by describing how God wanted Jonah to go to the important city of Nineveh and tell Israel's archenemies, the Assyrians, to repent of their wicked ways. "The ancient Assyrians were not your run-of-the-mill enemy. They were powerful, brutal, and relentless in their hatred towards the Israelites. If you ever have a chance, take a look at ancient Assyrian art. Some of their murals depict what they did to their opponents, and I'll tell you, they make the movie Braveheart look like a picnic. They were nasty, hateful people, and God wanted Jonah to go by himself and tell them so.

"So Jonah knew just what God wanted him to do, but he

didn't want to do it. Would you? Jonah forgot that God doesn't give us a job to do without helping us do it. Jonah felt he couldn't obey God because he had forgotten to trust God.

"Jonah was so afraid that he tried to outsmart and outrun God. In fact, he boarded a ship headed in the opposite direction from Nineveh! Today it would be like God asking you to go talk some sense into Saddam Hussein, but instead you hop on a plane to, say, Rio. I think you get the picture.

"As we pick up the story in chapter 1, verse 4, Jonah thinks he's safe once he's on board the ship, so he goes below deck to get some sleep. Everything is going according to plan. Then God sends a storm that threatens both the ship and the lives of everyone on board. The sailors frantically try to save the ship, but to no avail. They eventually suspect there might be some other reason for the storm. They confront Jonah, who reveals that he is an Israelite running away from the Lord. He also admits that he must be the reason for the storm. The sailors are now terrified, and the storm is getting worse. Jonah finally tells them to throw him overboard since the whole thing is his fault. And when they do throw him overboard, the sea grows calm. But that's not the end of Jonah; God sent a great fish to swallow him, and he stayed inside the fish for three days and three nights, praying and asking God for another chance.

"Now, get ready folks, because here comes Principle Four: *Nothing will begin to improve in your life until you are willing to make the changes necessary to improve yourself.* Jonah's life begins to turn around only when he recognizes his mistake, asks God to forgive him, and promises to change. He realizes that only God can help him out of his situation, so he promises to do things God's way from now on. And once Jonah makes that decision, things begin to look up. Immediately! God commands the fish to spit Jonah up onto dry land. And the rest is all history: Jonah obeyed, went to Nineveh, and was used by God to turn a whole city around."

Ray turned off the tape and wrote: *If things are going to improve, I have to be willing to change first.* He read the sentence over and over. *If things are going to improve, I have to be willing to change first.* "But I'm not even sure what changes I have to make," he said tiredly.

He began to think it through, creating a dialogue in his head. *So, okay, say I'm willing to change, but what changes do I have to make? I'm a nice person: smart, honest, a good husband and father. What do I have in common with Jonah? I've studied at good schools, I've worked hard, and I have a good job. I've earned a lovely home and have a nice family. I've even started going to a good church. Everything was going according to plan until this happened. Everything was going according to plan.*

Ray heard the echo of the sermon in his own thoughts. *Jonah thought his life was going according to plan, too, but it was the wrong plan. Jonah's problem was that he was ignoring God's plan.* Ray froze. *So here I am, living my life according to my plan, Mr. MBA who knows a thing or two, without even considering that the creator of the universe might have a better plan. I've been too smart, too sensible, and too self-sufficient to waste time on God. I'm worse than Jonah. He disobeyed, but at least he was listening.*

Ray began to speak quietly. "God, I've ignored you most of my life. Even deciding to go to church this month was a measure to satisfy my agenda, not yours. I don't know if you sent this storm into my life now, but you definitely have my attention. So here I am in this hospital room, in the belly of *my* big fish. Please give *me* another chance. I'll change. I'll do anything, but please let Lindsey get better. Nothing else matters—not even my job. Just let her get better."

He didn't have any tears left, breathing for him felt like the dry heaves of crying today. He had promised to change, and he meant it, but he still didn't know exactly what that meant. Looking back over the story of Jonah, he figured that the prophet's first mistake was not trusting God. That was a place to start at least. But how could Ray really trust God? "Please show me how to trust You," he whispered.

Ray reached up to remove the earphones from his head and glanced over at Lindsey. She was just the same, motionless, almost lifeless. But then, just for a second, her eyes flickered open. They met Ray's gaze and then closed again.

11

Not until Wednesday did Ray leave Lindsey and return to work. The doctors had not shared Ray's optimism about Lindsey's brief awakening. Coma victims often seemed to revive briefly. Some people woke up and even spoke, before promptly sinking back into a coma. Often they died.

Ray hadn't told anyone about asking God to show him how to trust and how Lindsey's brief awakening afterwards seemed like an answer. It would sound too bizarre, and most people would just think it was a coincidence. But there had been too many coincidences in Ray's life recently. Ray couldn't explain it, but he knew now that God was there—that He was listening to him, that He cared. It wasn't about religion or choosing a system of belief. Ray just knew, and that knowing was the beginning of trust.

As it turned out, the doctors were correct. Lindsey had remained in a coma and had not stirred since Sunday night. Ray hated to leave her even for a few hours, but the doctors said there was nothing he could do there. Although it was hard for Ray to accept, life went on outside the hospital, even at Megna. There was nothing for him to do but go back to work. Gloria promised to beep him the moment there was any change in Lindsey.

When Ray entered the Megna Electronics building on Wednesday, people surrounded him showing their concern for Lindsey.

"How's your daughter, Ray?" asked Al Packard.

"She's still in a coma, but the fact that she opened her eyes gives us hope. Thanks for asking."

"I'll keep her in my prayers."

"Thanks," said Ray as he walked towards his office. *Funny, he thought to himself, I would have never thought of Al as a praying man. But then, Al probably thinks the same thing about me.* Ray also remembered what he had prayed in Lindsey's hospital room. *I'll change. Just give me another chance.* That promise no longer seemed so daunting.

Megna needed to change too. Immediately. The days Ray had missed had put them all behind in meeting the goals John had given the Activity-Based Costing Team the previous week. Ray was glad to have Principle Four under his belt, though. Although he knew he would never forget it, he had summarized it on one of his note cards: *Nothing will improve in your life unless you are willing to change.*

Just as he knew he had to change personally, Ray was convinced that Megna also had to change the way it did things. It was time to take decisive action. He picked up the phone and called Kathi. "Can you round up your team and meet in my office in fifteen minutes?"

"Sure. What's up?"

"It's time to change ABC from a noun to a verb." said Ray.

"Huh?"

"I'll explain when you get everyone rounded up." Ray hung up and arranged the papers on his desk.

Five seconds later the phone rang. "Ray, it's Chris. Do you have an answer yet on the Greenbelt issue? I've got to get back to them this week about their request for lower prices."

Ray had forgotten all about the meeting with Chris Meyers and his promise to see if the activity-based cost information would shed any light on Greenbelt's profitability. "Gee, Chris, I'm sorry. I've been wrapped up in so many other things that I forgot. But I promise to get you an answer by the end of the week."

"Okay, fine," said Chris.

Ray was kicking himself mentally as Kathi and her team came in and sat down. After answering their questions about Lindsey, he got down to business.

"Folks, we need to come up with an action plan, one that will convert our ABC findings into results on the P&L. John says we need to show how we can achieve a ten-percent profit improvement in ninety days, and none of the departments seem to be making any progress on their own."

"That's a lot of money in a little time," said Dick, and the others nodded.

"You're right, but John is simply responding to demands from headquarters. If Megna can't provide a reasonable return on their investment, they will sell us, transfer our products offshore, or close us down. None of those options is particularly appealing to me . . . and probably not to you either. So let's give it our best shot and see what we can do as a team."

Everyone agreed, so Ray continued. "Great. So let's plan the work and then work the plan," said Ray, smiling, as he walked towards the greaseboard on the office wall. "We can't come up with all the ideas to reduce costs ourselves, our team is too small. We need to find a way to get everyone at Megna involved."

"We may be few in number," Dick added, "but we know the ABC data better than anyone, and we've got some pretty creative people on this team. I bet we can come up with the cost improvements we need on our own."

"You're right, Dick, but let me show you the power of multiplication," said Ray.

"What do you mean?"

"Look," said Ray, "if we implemented ABC in only one department, focused on one activity, had one improvement plan worth $1,000 per month, and implemented that idea for one month, how much would we save?" Ray wrote $1 \times 1 \times 1 \times \$1,000 \times 1 =$ on the board.

Dick said, "Obviously the answer is we'd save $1,000."

"Right," said Ray. "Now, what if we changed every one to a two. How much would we improve?"

"Okay," said Dick, "If we had two departments, with two activities per department, and two improvements worth $2,000 per month for each activity, in two months we would save . . . $32,000."

"Okay, math whiz. What if we change each number to 3?"

This time, using the calculator, Dick said, "$243,000."

Number of Departments		Number of Activities		Number of Improvements		Value of each Improvement		Number of Months		Cost Savings
1	×	1	×	1	×	$1k	×	1	=	$1,000
2	×	2	×	2	×	$2k	×	2	=	$32,000
3	×	3	×	3	×	$3k	×	3	=	$243,000
4	×	4	×	4	×	$4k	×	4	=	$1,024,000

"Right again. If we increase it to 4, we'll hit the target headquarters has set for us. The key is to use the power of multiplication. We need to get people in every department to focus on improving their activities. If we're successful, there's no telling how profitable this company can be."

"That's exciting, Ray, but how? How do you propose we get every department to improve its activities?"

"Well, that's where I hope Valerie can help us out," said Ray. Valerie looked up, surprised.

"Valerie," continued Ray, "you mentioned how you've been implementing total quality management for two years. Refresh my memory. Isn't there a problem-solving process they use in TQM?"

"Yes, there is," she replied. "It's a five-step improvement process. Step 1 is to identify the problem. Step 2 is to define the root causes of the problem. Step 3 is to identify solutions for the root cause. Step 4 is to implement the best solution. And Step 5 is to measure the results."

Ray wrote each of the five steps on the board as Valerie stated them. Then he said, "Okay, let's start with step 1: identify the problem. I think each of Megna's departments can use their activity accounting spreadsheet to help identify problems and improvement opportunities. The spreadsheet shows them their non-value waste, high-cost activities, and high-workload activities."

"I agree," said Janis, who was usually quiet in these sessions. "I've had the TQM training, and we already use these five steps for problem solving in my department. I'd recommend that each department use a fish-bone diagram or storyboarding session to list all the root causes of an activity for step 2."

"You're losing me," said Dick. "I don't know what you're talking about."

"Oh, sorry," said Janis. "I'm talking about two visual tools for problem analysis. The Japanese use a diagram that displays cause and effect factors related to specific problem areas. They draw the results as a bunch of intersecting lines. The diagram actually looks like a fish bone, hence the name. Storyboarding or the Five-Whys technique are something else you can do to understand the root cause of activities. I have some books in my office that explain them. You can stop by and I'll show them to you later, if you want."

"That's a great idea," said Valerie. "I'm glad someone is actually using the TQM training. Along the same lines, the best source for solutions in step 3 would be the employees who perform the activities. Maybe they could brainstorm to come up with ideas and then pick the best one."

"Good," said Ray. "What do you recommend for step 4?"

Dick said, "I think that each department should estimate the impact of its improvement plan on their activity accounting spreadsheet. In other words, what is the cost of the activity both *before* the change and *after* the change? The before and after comparison will tell us the cost savings."

"Absolutely, Dick," said Kathi. "And the spreadsheet will be an easy way to measure achievement of the improvement plan in step 5."

"All right, we have a plan and a method." said Ray, a little surprised at how quickly it had come together. "Now, for the hard part, how do we work the plan?"

Valerie spoke up. "How about if each member of the team selects a department to work with. I don't think it will take more than a couple of days, maybe four hours on one day to cover steps 1, 2, and 3, and then a few more hours the next day to complete steps 4 and 5. We'd have to train them how to read, interpret, and use the spreadsheet. But the remaining steps should be pretty straightforward once they've selected an activity to improve."

"I like it," said Ray. "Now, let's not forget that we'll be asking people to find new ways of doing things. We'll need to remind them that, to improve, Megna has to change. Sometimes it's hard to give up old habits, but we've got to convince them we can't expect improved results this year if we use last year's activities and last year's methods."

"Got it," said Kathi and everyone nodded. Before they left, they each selected a department to work with. Ray told everyone to report their improvement ideas back to him by the following Monday. As they filed out of the office, Ray called Kathi back.

"Before you get started working with your department, I need your help in answering a pricing and profitability question for Chris Meyers."

"Sure. What do you need?" said Kathi.

"I need the activity accounting reports for every department."

"How will they answer Chris's pricing question?"

Ray walked to his greaseboard and wrote three words: *Activities consume resources.* "These three words are the basic foundation of what we've done so far, right?"

"Now that I think about it, it is that simple."

Ray then picked up the pen again and wrote three more words: *Customers consume activities.* "It just came to me when I was writing the multiplication formula on the board for Dick. If I can determine how much of each activity is consumed by each customer or product, I can more accurately allocate our labor and overhead costs. Does that make sense to you?"

"Well, it sounds more complicated than the way we allocate overhead now. But, from what you've just said, allocating activities instead of an overhead rate sounds more accurate. What do you need me to do?"

"The only thing I need right now are the spreadsheets. Later I may need you and Dick to help, but not yet."

"Okay, I'll get them to you later this morning." Kathi started to leave, but then she turned back. "What was it you said about turning ABC from a noun into a verb? I don't get it."

"What I meant was that until now, ABC just reported the facts. Information is useful only if you put it to good use. Understanding costs is one thing, but using cost information to manage the business is another. Cost is a noun, manage is a verb. In fact, I think what we're doing here is turning into something more than just activity-based costing. Now that we've moved into the realm of action, I think of it as activity-based management: ABM."

"I think I follow you, Ray. So, now that we're actually using the spreadsheets to help the company change, I guess we should start calling ourselves the ABM Team."

"Whatever," said Ray as Kathi left. It didn't really make much difference to him what they called it, he just wanted to move the project ahead and see some improvement in the bottom line.

Ray sighed and leaned back in his chair. *So much for Megna . . . now what activities in my life need to be improved?* he pondered. Ray knew he didn't have a spreadsheet for his personal activities, so instead he pulled a blank sheet of paper from his desk drawer. He drew a line down the middle. On the left side, he listed all the things he enjoyed doing, like playing golf, playing with the kids, and shopping on Saturday with Gloria. On the right side he wrote down all the things he hated doing, like working overtime, long business trips, and driving in heavy traffic. As he picked up the phone to check on Lindsey, he wondered what it would take to shift more time from the right to the left.

12

Ray visited the hospital each day, and he and Gloria traded off staying through the night. As the week went by, more cards and flowers arrived, but there were fewer visitors. This troubled Ray and Gloria, at first, but then they figured most people had their own lives and problems to deal with. They decided to be thankful that people came when they did.

David was still staying with Sandy and her husband, which gave Ray and Gloria the freedom to stay as late as they wanted at the hospital. "They're so great. We really owe them," Gloria had said.

Sandy took David to school each day and picked him up in the afternoon. Although David had adjusted to these changes, he was ready to go back to his own house, sleep in his own bed, and play with his own toys. Ray was able to take him to McDonald's for dinner one night, but most evenings, David was asleep by the time Ray got home. David didn't ask about Lindsey very often. When he did, he wanted to know when she was coming home.

Gloria practically lived at the hospital. She kept a daily journal of who had visited, what thoughts she had had, and what the doctors had said. She had already started on her second notebook in the one week since Lindsey had been admitted.

Ray tried to bury himself in his work, but he found the daily contact with other people a strain. Everyone meant well, but no one could really understand what he was going through. People at the office, vendors, sales people, anyone who came by or ran into Ray seemed resigned that Lindsey wasn't going to make it.

"We're so sorry, Mr. Miller," they'd say. "If there's anything we can do, let us know."

If there's anything you can do? Ray wanted to scream. *I'll tell you what you can do! You can stop being so somber and negative. My daughter's going to be fine. She's going to be fine, and she doesn't need you to write her off.* Ray wanted to shake every person who spoke to him, but he kept his thoughts to himself instead and thanked them all for their concern.

As if dealing with daily condolences wasn't enough, Ray's closest friends had put pressure on him to sue the driver of the truck. Glenn, an attorney and old friend, and Bill double-teamed him at lunch one day and suggested that he go after the driver and the delivery company. Ray knew their intentions were good and that they just didn't want to see his family ruined by hospital bills, but he wasn't interested.

It was all so confusing. Glenn and Bill had said he had a good case, but the image of Lindsey, still bruised and unconscious, the prospect of the unpleasantness of litigation, and the punishment of the faceless people who were liable for the accident played like a bad movie in his head. He didn't want anger to drive his decisions. He didn't want to punish anyone, and he didn't want revenge. He just wanted his daughter back. Why couldn't people understand that?

There had been no change in Lindsey's condition all week. Since Sunday she'd made no progress at all. By Friday evening, the strain of the whole week was wearing on both Ray and Gloria. It was only seven days since the accident, but they could hardly remember what life had been like before. As she did every night, Gloria filled Ray in on who had called and who had come by.

Lindsey had a new visitor that day, the youth minister at Calvary Bible Church. Gloria said she was sorry Lindsey's eyes were closed because the minister was so good looking. She and Ray both started to laugh, but the laughter got stuck in their throats and tears came instead. During the past week, they both had learned to compose themselves quickly. Gloria blinked hard and went on. She told Ray how nice the young man had been to her and how he had prayed with Lindsey. "You would have liked him, Ray. He has hope too. He talked to Lindsey as if she could hear him and said he was saving a place for her in the youth group." It amazed them both that not one, but two pastors had made the effort to come, and the Millers weren't even members of the church.

Ray had wanted to take David to a ball game Saturday, but Gloria needed to get away from the hospital for a while, so instead, she stayed home and Ray and David went to the hospital. David brought some comic books and cards. They played Go Fish and Slap Jack until David got bored. Then Ray let him go down to the vending machines and buy Cokes and candy, his normal parental strictness melting in the face of guilt and fatigue.

The afternoon sun angled in and set the hospital room aglow. David fell asleep in a chair as Ray tried to catch up on the newspaper. He felt like he'd lost touch with the whole world this week. The phone began to ring and Ray intercepted it quickly before it woke David. It was Rev. Owens calling to check on the family. He asked if it was all right for him to stop by Sunday afternoon and offered to bring a tape of the morning service. Ray was grateful for the offer. He hated to miss church, but he knew his place was at Lindsey's bedside this week. He realized now that it wasn't just Principle Five he wanted to hear; he wanted to stay connected to this church. The tape would help.

Gloria and Ray were both in the room when Rev. Owens came by Sunday. They felt a little awkward as they weren't used to being around ministers. They were afraid they might say something wrong or sacrilegious without knowing it. But Rev. Owens quickly put them at ease. He was friendly and not pushy, and he left before they had a chance to say anything embarrassing. Soon after, Gloria went to pick up David from Sandy's. She wanted to give him some "mommy time" before the next week got underway.

Alone again, Ray put on the headphones, slipped the sermon tape into Lindsey's Walkman, and leaned back, his eyes closed. The music sounded a little wobbly on the recording, but the sermon came through clearly.

"This morning," said Rev. Owens, "we continue our series of ten life-changing principles. Let's turn in our Bibles to Genesis, chapter 37. Here we meet one of the greatest characters in all of the Bible. His name is Joseph.

"If you've ever had problems in your life, you're going to like Joseph. If you've ever been mistreated or betrayed, falsely accused or lied about, cheated or wronged, you're going to like him. If you've ever faced impossible circumstances or found yourself in a terrible situation, you're going to love Joseph. Because, in the face of his troubles, he did what was right and ended up on top."

Sounds like my kind of guy, Ray thought.

Rev. Owens took the congregation on a historical tour of Joseph's troubles. "Joseph was the next to youngest of Jacob's twelve sons, and he was Jacob's favorite. Jacob didn't make any secret of his preference. In fact, he gave Joseph a 'richly ornamented' robe to show his special love. The Bible doesn't call it a technicolor dreamcoat—Andrew Lloyd Weber came up with that—but we can be certain that it was special and visibly demonstrated his favoritism. Of course, sibling rivalry isn't a twenty-first-century invention. As you can imagine, his brothers were jealous—they hated him."

Ray squirmed a little, thinking of how little attention he had given to David recently. He made a mental note to try harder next week.

Rev. Owens's voice went on. "Joseph's brothers decided to kill him, but instead, at the last minute, they sold him to some slave traders traveling to Egypt. In Egypt, Joseph was sold to Potiphar, the captain of the guard in Pharaoh's house. How would you feel if your brothers did that to you? Talk about dysfunctional families! Today it's the kind of things you unfortunately hear on daytime talk shows.

"But we have no record of Joseph bad-mouthing his brothers. Instead, he accepted his situation, went to work, and did his job well. It was the right thing to do, and God blessed Joseph and everything in Potiphar's household. Things were beginning to look up. But then Potiphar's wife became interested in Joseph. When Joseph didn't succumb to her advances, she falsely accused him of trying to rape her. Potiphar had him thrown into prison.

"But even in prison, God was with him. Instead of despairing,

Joseph chose to do other things with his time. God gave Joseph the opportunity to help a cupbearer who had served in Pharaoh's household by interpreting some very important dreams for him. The cupbearer promised to help Joseph when he was released from prison, but he didn't. The cupbearer completely forgot about Joseph.

"Finally, after a couple of years went by, Joseph interpreted some dreams for Pharaoh himself. Pharaoh was so impressed by Joseph that he released him from prison and made him his second-in-command. Once Joseph was in a position of great power, he could have spent his time taking revenge on the cupbearer or following his own goals. He could have thrown Potiphar's wife in jail. He could have devised a plan to destroy Egypt's economy, effectively damaging a country that had taken so much of his life away. Instead, he went about storing up the country's grain so all of Egypt would have plenty to eat when a famine he had foreseen came.

"And what about Joseph's brothers? When the food ran out in their country, they came to Egypt for help. Would we have blamed Joseph for turning them away? Instead, he showed them kindness and gave them help.

"Here was a man who had lost everything, faced impossible circumstances, undergone incredible temptations, and yet he never retaliated. It wasn't fair of his brothers to get rid of him just because his father loved him more. It wasn't fair that he was thrown in jail, an innocent man who had helped his accuser's house prosper. It wasn't fair that the cupbearer he helped reneged on his promise. Joseph had every reason to turn his back on Egypt and his family when he had the chance. But he never sought revenge. He never fought back. He never sought his own way. Instead of demanding his rights, he simply did what was right. He didn't allow the behavior of others to keep him from doing what was right.

"Joseph illustrates the fifth principle I want to share with you this morning. Are you ready? *It's never wrong to do what's right and never right to do what's wrong.* Joseph was a success. He was rewarded by God because he refused to cut corners in any area of his life.

He refused to give in to pressure. He refused to seek his own rights when he'd been wronged. He did exactly what he was supposed to do—let the chips fall where they might—and left the outcome of his life up to God."

After the week Ray had just experienced, this was a message he needed to hear. He'd faced so much pressure and endured so much stress. Talk about impossible situations! His daughter lay comatose in a hospital bed just a few feet away. He'd been counseled to fight back, to get what was rightfully his by filing a lawsuit. He'd been so confused. But Rev. Owens had helped clear his perspective again.

Do the right thing, no matter what. he wrote on the card. And in large capital letters he wrote: IT'S NEVER WRONG TO DO WHAT'S RIGHT AND NEVER RIGHT TO DO WHAT'S WRONG. Ray knew immediately that for him, suing wouldn't make things right, and it wouldn't be right. It was a relief just to be able to think clearly about it. As for doing the right thing at Megna, he'd have to think about that some more.

13

"Ray, we're going to strike unless Megna can guarantee our jobs," said Al Packard, who seemed a little uncomfortable in his role as shop steward.

"What?" Ray couldn't believe what he was hearing. When he had agreed to meet with Al and Mary Forsman again, he had assumed that they simply wanted an update on the ABM project. The ABM overview session for the employees had gone well, and he had heard that everyone seemed to be cooperating.

It isn't enough, Ray thought, *that I put my career on the line with a new approach, that I'm working like mad, and that I'm somehow trying to deal with having my daughter in the hospital indefinitely? I really don't need to hear about an impending strike to add more stress to my life. How much can a person stand?"*

"I don't understand, Al. What do you mean?"

"You've got a team of people going around to every department asking employees for cost-cutting ideas."

"Right, Al. We've talked about this. We need improvement ideas and we need them now."

"You may need the ideas, but we're not going to give them to you. The union members are not going to participate in these meetings unless Megna guarantees our jobs."

"But, Al, you know there are no guarantees in life, except maybe death and taxes."

"Well, I'll just add one more to your list," said Al. "I guarantee you that the union will not participate in this ABM project of yours unless our jobs are guaranteed."

Ray looked to Mary for help. "Mary, what do you think about all this?" he asked.

"I don't see how Megna Electronics, or any company for that matter, can guarantee lifetime employment. But I do think we should give everyone some idea of management's plans and priorities," said Mary.

"We all know the plan, Mary," said Ray. "Isn't that what our overview session was all about? We've got to improve profits and do it quickly or we're all going to be out of a job."

"Wait a minute," exploded Al. "What do you mean we'll all be out of a job?" He got up, looked at both Ray and Mary with disgust, and walked to the door. "I want John Brady to meet with me and all the union employees and I want to meet with him sooner rather than later." Al announced. "And I want to hear from his lips a job guarantee as well as his plans for this company's future. Until I hear that from him, we're not participating in your ABM meetings." Al closed the door behind him.

"Great," said Ray. "Here we are trying to turn the company around and the union threatens a walkout. I call that teamwork!"

"I know, Ray, it's terrible timing, but I have to say I think Al makes a valid point," commented Mary.

"You think we should guarantee their jobs?" Ray asked, staring at her.

"No, I didn't say that, but I sense that their mistrust stems from not knowing what we plan to do with the non-value waste we've identified. Somehow I'd like to be able to assure them that cutting waste doesn't necessarily mean cutting jobs, and that laying people off is not what we have in mind."

"I'll tell you exactly what we have in mind," said Ray, "to improve the bottom line, and fast. But we can't have our hands tied by unrealistic guarantees."

"Ray, if I remember my Accounting 101 class from college, there's more than one way to improve the bottom line. You can increase sales, reduce costs, or fiddle around with both. You did a good job of explaining ABM cost analysis to the employees, and I believe they understand that it's a useful tool. But now we're back into cost-cutting mode, and that has always meant one thing to them: layoffs. I think we need to develop a general list of improvement options—for example, increase volume, improve margins, or both—get John's approval, and have him talk to the workers. If they understand what we're up against, maybe they'll work with us."

Ray knew Mary's recommendation would help. He thought again about Principle Five: *It's never wrong to do what's right and never right to do what's wrong.* "Okay," he acknowledged, "and maybe we'll do more than just placate the workers. Looking at the non-value waste again might help us focus on doing the right things too. I'd hate to be doing a great job of cutting the wrong costs."

Mary smiled. "All right. Why don't you work up a plan to show John? Call me if you need some help. In the meantime, I've got an idea for a plan that might help the employees feel better about improvement. I'm going back to my office to put it down on paper. Okay?"

"Well, I don't have a better plan, so let's proceed. I'll call and let you know if we can meet with John later today," said Ray as Mary got up to leave.

Ray closed his office door. He thought again about Principle Five and Joseph as he walked back to his desk. How could he ever be that good? Not only did Joseph do the right thing, he never wasted time venting his anger or getting back at people, despite all his troubles. Instead, he redirected his energy to thinking right and acting right.

But that's it! thought Ray. *Why didn't I think of it before? If we can come up with ideas to redirect our energy and our resources, including labor, from non-value to value, we could probably improve profits without cutting jobs.* Ray jumped out of his chair and grabbed a grease pen. At the top of his greaseboard he wrote, *What to do with the Non-Value-Added Waste.*

Ray wrote the options in order of priority, based on which ones would be most likely to save jobs and increase profits:

1. Use excess resources to fund value activities in the department where the excess is found.
2. Use excess resources to fund value activities in other departments.

3. Use excess resources to fund new activities anywhere in the organization—e.g., new products.
4. Use excess resources in departments that can increase sales revenue.
5. Eliminate excess resources over time through attrition.
6. Eliminate excess resources immediately.

As Ray stepped back to review the list, Gloria called.

"Ray, it's me. No change." Ray had asked Gloria to call every day at noon to let him know how things were going at the hospital.

He could hear the depression in her voice. As they talked, Ray thought, *Why do bad things happen to good people? My life's a mess. My daughter is in a coma in the hospital. My company is in turmoil. And everyone is looking to me for the answers. My wife, my boss, my fellow workers. I just don't know how long I can keep doing this.*

"Rev. Owens just dropped by the hospital again," said Gloria.

"That's nice." The mention of his name reminded Ray of something Rev. Owens had told him the day before.

"Ray," the pastor had said, "I know you're worried about Lindsey. But did you know that God doesn't want us to worry? Worrying means we don't trust him." It occurred to Ray that worrying was a non-value activity. But to him it was a forty-year habit. It took more discipline than he had at that moment not to worry about it all, but he resolved to add worrying to the list of ways he had to change.

Ray promised to come by the hospital after work before hanging up. The phone rang again. This time it was Mary.

"Ray," she said excitedly, "I just got off the phone with a friend of mine. I hope you don't mind, but I told him about our cost-reduction plan. He told me about a continuous improvement program he implemented at his company two years ago. I think it might work for us. Do you have a minute for me to come by and explain it to you?"

"Sure, come on down. Kathi and Chris are due here pretty soon, but we can talk until they get here."

When Mary arrived, she studied the six options Ray had written on the board. Ray explained, "I realized that waste represents what happens when we spend some of our resources doing the wrong things. We can't afford to be doing the wrong things, even if we're doing them well. We need to use all of our resources, not just some of them, doing the right things—things that will improve our bottom line. That's what I tried to do here—find more profitable ways to use our resources."

Mary agreed that they looked reasonable to her. While the options did not guarantee jobs, the list did show that every attempt would be made to prevent layoffs. Assuming that John Brady would approve it later in the day, Mary recommended John explain the options to the employees through a series of meetings. Ray agreed.

"So, what's this new idea?" Ray asked curiously.

"Well, my friend has a simple program that generates three to four hundred cost improvement ideas per month," said Mary.

"You must be kidding!" exclaimed Ray. "How does he do it?"

"Like I said, the program is really quite simple, but it won't work unless everyone agrees that we need to change the way we do things. Your options here on the board will help."

"Okay. So how does it work?" said Ray.

"Well, if an employee turns in any continuous improvement idea, they get a coin. It's not real money, just a token or a colored chip. If the idea is approved by management and then implemented, the employee gets two more coins. And when you accumulate three coins, you can turn them in for a prize."

"Wait a minute. Don't they calculate the cost savings before handing out the coins?" asked Ray.

"They used to, but the person who calculated the cost savings became the most hated person in the company. The employees always complained that the estimate was too low, and management always complained that the savings estimate was too high. The poor estimator couldn't win."

"So what do they do with the coins?"

"Here's the beauty of the program. Every Friday morning at ten, the president of the company goes to the cafeteria. All employees are encouraged to take a break for fifteen minutes and join him there. Anyone who has three coins steps forward, one at a time, and hands them to the president. As the employee does this, everyone else applauds, so the employee gets recognized for his contribution."

"It sounds good, but are you telling me the employees are turning in improvement ideas just to get applause?"

"That's part of it, but there's more. After giving their coins to the president, the employee gets to spin a giant prize wheel—kind of like a Wheel of Fortune. But instead of money, each prize on the wheel involves the employee's family."

"Say what? You mean they don't want cash?" Ray had trouble believing that.

"They used to give away cash, but they found that employees would forget about their winnings by the next week. You know, they'd apply the cash against a credit card bill or buy groceries or something, then forget about the continuous improvement program. So now, every prize on the wheel benefits the winner's family—things like dinner for four at a local restaurant, tickets to a ball game, or admission for the whole family to an amusement park."

"It sounds nice but why is that better than cash?" asked Ray.

"It's brilliant," said Mary, "because it creates continuous improvement in stereo. Not only do the employees hear about improvement at work, but now, when they go home, their kids say 'Dad, did you turn in any ideas this week? We want to go to the ball game again!' "

"So they're averaging close to four hundred ideas a month just because of this prize wheel?"

"No, it's not just about the prizes, Ray. It all starts with everyone agreeing that improvement is seriously needed. You give employees the tools, the training, and the targets, then let them run with it. The prizes are just a reward. We've already given our employees the tool they need: It's called ABM. And your ABM team is already giving training on how to use ABM to identify cost-saving opportunities. I'm convinced that if John is open and honest with all the employees about our profit improvement target and shows them your six options for dealing with waste, we can get the same kind of response from our employees."

"I hope you're right," Ray concluded. "Let's tell John all about it this afternoon. But right now I can see Chris and Kathi waiting for me outside the door."

"Next!" Ray called as Mary left and Chris and Kathi came in. "Do you know the difference between stupidity and genius?" Ray queried.

Kathi and Chris shook their heads.

Solving the riddle, Ray answered, "Genius has its limits, stupidity doesn't," Chris and Kathi laughed, as Ray added, "and I'm approaching my limit. I hope you're not here looking for a solution to another crisis."

"Well," Kathi responded, "I have some good news and some bad news." Which do you want first?"

Chris interrupted. "Wait, here's one I just heard. A man got a call from his wife. She says, 'Honey, I have some good news and some bad news. Which do you want first?' The man's had a hard day so he says, 'Just give me the good news.' His wife pauses for a moment and says, 'Well, the good news is that both air bags on our new Lexus work.'"

Ray laughed. "Sounds like my morning. So what's the good news, Kathi?"

"Well, here's the situation. Greenbelt Computer wants us to reduce our prices. With our current profit-improvement program, reducing prices seems counterproductive."

"No kidding," said Chris.

"Ray, you gave me three words of advice to approach this issue: *Customers consume activities.* Since you're swamped with other things both here and at the hospital, I went ahead and looked at the activity accounting spreadsheets myself. Looking at the rows of expenses and the columns of activities, I had an idea. Why not create another spreadsheet, but this time, put the activities in the rows and customers in the columns?"

Kathi handed Chris and Ray a customer profitability analysis for Greenbelt Computer and explained her approach. "First I sat down with the departmental managers and asked them if any of their activities were directly consumed by Greenbelt. If they answered yes, I asked them how many outputs of each activity were traceable to Greenbelt."

"You had time to sit down with every department manager and gather that data?" said Ray.

"No, I didn't. I looked at our ABM findings and noticed that twenty percent of our activities consume eighty percent of our monthly costs. So I focused on those activities."

"That makes sense, but is it true? Roughly thirty activities consume eighty percent of our labor and overhead costs? What else did you find out?"

"Ray, you won't believe how much interesting data there is in the ABM database Dick created, but let's get back to Greenbelt. I asked employees like those who work with Chris in order processing, 'What activities in your department are consumed by Greenbelt?' I quickly learned our employees had all the information that we needed. For example, let's look at the report I just handed you."

Chris and Ray opened their copies. Chris said, "Kathi, I'm sorry to jump ahead, but if I read the lower right column correctly, you're saying that Megna Electronics is losing money by selling to Greenbelt. How is that possible?"

"Good question, Chris," said Kathi. "Let me walk you through what I did. Greenbelt purchased $50,000 worth of product from us this year. The products they purchased cost us $25,000 to manufacture. That includes raw material, labor, and manufacturing overhead."

"What do you mean by manufacturing overhead?" asked Chris.

"That includes departments like Receiving, Purchasing, and Quality Assurance," said Kathi.

"I got it. Go ahead."

"Looking at the ABM findings, I found that twenty percent of the activities consume eighty percent of our costs, just like I said. So I met with every department that had one or more of the most expensive activities. I asked each manager or supervisor, 'How many of your department's activities are consumed by Greenbelt?'"

"And why didn't you sit down with every department?" asked Chris.

"For two reasons. First, I had to get this analysis done quickly, there wasn't time. Second, because of the 80/20 analysis, there really was no need to meet with everyone."

Activities Consume Resources

Order Processing Department	Take Orders VA	Expedite Orders NVA	Change Orders NVA	Issue Credits NVA	Answer Inquiries VA	Manage Employees VA
Salary/Fringes	$460,000	$248,000	$60,000	$62,000	$67,000	$6,000	$17,000
Space	50,000	20,000	5,000	7,000	5,000	3,000	10,000
Depreciation	50,000	20,000	2,000	10,000	4,000	10,000	4,000
Supplies	30,000	10,000	2,000	10,000	3,000	1,000	4,000
Other	10,000	2,000	1,000	1,000	1,000	0	5,000
Total	$600,000	$300,000	$70,000	$90,000	$80,000	$20,000	$40,000
Output Measure		10,000 Orders	1,000 Expedites	2,000 Changes	4,000 Credits	4,000 Calls	15 People
Cost per Output		$30	$70	$45	$20	$5	$2,666

Customers Consume Activities

Greenbelt ABC Customer Profitability Analysis

	Value	Non-Value	Total
Sales	$50,000	$0	$50,000
Cost of Goods	$25,000	$0	$25,000
Gross Margin	$25,000	$0	$25,000
	50%		50%

	Output				
Activity	Quantity	Cost	Value	Non-Value	Total
Take Orders	100	$30	$3,000	$0	$3,000
Expedite Orders	50	$70	0	3,500	3,500
Change Orders	25	$45	0	1,125	1,125
Issue Credits	30	$20	0	600	600
Answer Inquiries	70	$5	350	0	350
Pick/Pack	100	$20	2,000	0	2,000
Deliver Order	100	$65	6,500	0	6,500
Issue Invoice	100	$10	1,000	0	1,000
Process Payments	100	$5	500	0	500
Receive Returns	30	$20	0	600	600
Issue Credits	30	$5	0	150	150
Procure Goods	100	$25	2,000	500	2,500
Non-Traceable Activities	100	$50	3,250	1,750	5,000
Total Activity Cost			$18,600	$8,225	$26,825
Pre-Tax Profit			$6,400	<$8,225>	<$1,825>
			12%	<16%>	<4%>

"Makes sense," said Chris. "Can you take me through what you did in Order Processing? They report to me, so I'm pretty familiar with what they do."

"Sure," said Kathi. "Look at the activity, 'Take Orders.' The spreadsheet shows that Order Processing processed 10,000 orders for all our customers. Since it cost us $300,000 to take orders, the cost per order is $30. Sue, the department supervisor, looked in her files and found that Greenbelt Computer placed one hundred orders to purchase $50,000 worth of our products. Since it costs $30 to take an order, I deducted $3,000 from Greenbelt's gross margin."

Ray jumped back into the discussion. "So you're saying that the other 9,900 orders were placed, or consumed, by other customers?"

"Yes," said Kathi. "I followed the same process for the other activities in the profitability analysis. For example, Greenbelt called us fifty times to expedite their orders. An expedite costs us $70, therefore, I multiplied fifty and seventy, equaling $3,500. But notice that I put the $3,500 in the non-value column. You see, I put the activity costs in the value or non-value columns, based on our employees' classifications."

"From what you describe, you've created a Bill of Activity." Ray observed. "In essence, the Bill of Activity works just like our Bill of Material ... purchase price times quantity consumed equals total cost. Purchase price in the ABC Bill of Activity is the cost per output of the activity. Quantity equals the amount of each activity consumed. Makes sense to me."

"So you like it?" asked Kathi.

Ray quickly responded with "Absolutely! But what's the line you labeled 'Non-Traceable Activities'?"

"That line represents the cost of activities that I couldn't trace directly to this customer. Activities such as Do Monthly Closing, Do Housekeeping, and Do Budgets. I allocated a portion of these non-traceable activity costs to Greenbelt. To do that I added up the total costs of all non-traceable activities—$500,000—and then divided by the total number of orders—10,000. Since Greenbelt consumed 100 orders, I allocated to them $5,000 of the non-traceable costs."

"I can't say I have a better idea." Ray commented.

"This report says we lost $1,825 on the $50,000 of product we sold Greenbelt. That's awfully hard to believe," said Chris.

"I was surprised too," said Kathi, "but this ABM analysis provides a pretty clear picture of why we lost money on the Greenbelt account."

"So you're telling me we should decline Greenbelt's price reduction request?" asked Chris.

"That's what the report tells me," said Ray. "But you're the one who makes the big bucks around here. It's your decision."

"Looking at Kathi's analysis, I'm not even sure we should keep Greenbelt as a customer. We're losing money on them," murmured Chris. He looked at Kathi and then at Ray, hoping for an answer.

"Chris, you're closer to the customer than we are," replied Kathi, "but this report tells me we could be making $6,400 on their account if we were able to eliminate the non-value activity cost they consume."

"Okay. I get the hint from both of you. Let me take this report and see if I can come up with an answer that's a win/win for everyone," said Chris as he left. "Thanks for doing this, Kathi. At least it gives me some concrete facts to go on."

Kathi squinted. "Chris, are those turkeys on your tie?"

Chris said, "Look, I wore it because it's November, okay? It has nothing to do with Greenbelt." Kathi cracked up and Chris left in a hurry.

After Chris was gone, Ray said, "Kathi, you're going to have my job before this is all over with. You're doing a super job on this project. I can't thank you enough."

Kathi smiled and said, "Ray, I love working on this project. I haven't been this excited about work in I don't know how long. And I feel like it's pumping new energy into the rest of the company too."

"I hope you're right," said Ray. "By the way, how are the meetings with departments going? Any good cost improvement ideas coming out?"

"Yes, but it's another good news, bad news thing. I'll update you later."

"You're just going to leave me hanging?"

"You've got it," she said and left before Ray could ask any more questions.

14

Before Ray left the office at noon on Friday, he picked up his messages. Several were from vendors and sales reps, but there was one marked "personal" from a Mr. Allen. Although the name sounded familiar, he couldn't place it, so he stuffed it into his pocket for later. He felt a little guilty about leaving early, but there was really nothing else he could do. Besides, everyone had urged him to spend the afternoon with his family.

The week had passed quickly and chaotically. John Brady had been furious when he heard about the impending strike, but he had seen the wisdom of diffusing the situation with accurate information. John had some meetings out of town during the week, but he asked Ray to give him a crash course on ABM as soon as he returned Monday so he could speak about ABM knowledgeably and confidently to the employees.

Ray congratulated Mary on her idea of having John talk to them. "If you'd worked in human resources as long as I have," Mary had said, "you'd know that most people feel better about change when they know that it's not just some manager's or consultant's pet project. They're more likely to help when the head honcho is leading it and they know it's in their best interest to comply. And John's so good at rallying the troops, I just know he can pull it off." Ray agreed with her completely.

"But," Mary continued, "he can't just pay lip service to it. He needs to know what he's talking about if he's going to really lead change." Ray told her about the overview he planned to give John next Monday.

Preparing for the overview had given Ray the chance to think through the whole process and clarify things in his own mind. He was anxious to go over it all with John. Kathi was making some headway with cost reduction ideas, but she really needed the cooperation of all the employees, and John was the key.

But something else had been bothering him all week. When Bill had come by to raise the idea of suing the trucking company again, Ray had blown up at him. Since there were few people closer to him than Bill, it was especially disturbing that he, of all people, couldn't understand why Ray wasn't interested in suing. Ray regretted some of the things he had said, like calling Bill ignorant and unfeeling. He hadn't seen Bill since and really wanted to clear the matter with him.

As he entered the hospital, Ray thought about how strange it was that it felt familiar. He pushed through doors and turned corners here automatically, as if he were in his own home. Even the mingled smells of disinfectant and hospital food had become part of his routine experience, like the fragrance of the jasmine bush outside his front door, or the smell of the coffee machine at work.

He paused and braced himself before entering Lindsey's room. No matter how familiar the hospital had become, seeing Lindsey unconscious was still a shock to him every time he entered her room. In his mind, Lindsey was his healthy, smiling girl. He had not allowed his mental image of her to change, so the reality of her condition always took him aback. As he entered, Gloria looked up from her book.

"Hi, honey," she said.

"How's she doing?" Ray asked.

"No change," said Gloria. She got up and gave him a hug. Ray responded mechanically.

"I'm beat," he said. "I think I'll go home and take a shower. Then I'll come back and we can get something to eat."

"Oh," said Gloria. Ray had noticed an edge creeping into her voice lately but had tried to ignore it.

"What's wrong?" asked Ray, though he was too tired to really care.

"Oh, nothing," said Gloria bitterly. "You just go along now

and shower, maybe read the paper while you're at it. I'm not tired; I don't need a shower. In fact, while you've been slaving away at the office, I've just been having a grand time here, eating bonbons and watching TV."

"What's with you?" Ray snapped irritably.

"Never mind." Gloria said, turning away from him, "Just go on home."

"No," argued Ray, "I don't get this. What did I do?"

"It's just that I've been sitting here all day, all week, watching our Lindsey lay here motionless, lifeless, and I don't know if any of us will ever laugh again. And I take care of the bills, and answer letters, and write thank you notes and do anything else that will take my mind off the reality that she's not going to make it. And I think that just maybe I can hang on until you get here. Then you just pop in and skip out. Your life hasn't changed that much. You can escape to your office every day and pretend that everything's okay. But everything's not okay." She finished angrily.

"Wait a minute," said Ray. "I have to work. My job pays the bills. Do you think I don't want to be here with you and Lindsey? That I'm not feeling the stress of it all?"

"We're losing our daughter, Ray. The doctors can't do anything. We can't do anything. And I'm sick of everything." Gloria started to cry. "And as if that's not enough, Mr. Allen called from David's school and told me they're having trouble with him."

"Who's Mr. Allen?" Ray asked.

"Your son's principal."

"So what did David do?"

"Mr. Allen said he tried to call you at the office, but you weren't in. Where were you? Golfing?"

"That's a cheap shot!" Now Ray was angry.

"Ray, I've had it," Gloria said bitterly, "Lindsey's not going to make it, and I'm not sure we're going to make it either." She got up. "You stay, I'll go." Then she left, letting the door slam behind her.

"Where are you going?" Ray shouted. He looked over at Lindsey, instinctively worried about waking her, but she didn't move a muscle.

Gloria came back later with Sandy and David. They stayed

with Lindsey while Gloria and Ray hurried over to David's school. Gloria had called ahead and arranged to meet with Mr. Allen and David's teacher, Ms. Shaw, before they left for the weekend. Ms. Shaw said that David had become disruptive in the classroom. He had been using inappropriate language and had gotten in a scuffle with another kid on the playground. The day before, he had drawn on the floor with markers.

"We didn't want to add to your worries right now," said Mr. Allen, "but it's gotten to the point that we need to get you involved." Ms. Shaw said David was a good kid, but that he was out of control. It was plain David was crying out for attention and that above all, he needed more time with his parents. Both Ray and Gloria determined to give David what he needed, but silently they each blamed the other.

The whole weekend was a strain. Every time Ray and Gloria were together, there was an unspoken tension between them. Because they had agreed not to argue in front of David or Lindsey, they didn't speak much at all.

Ray thought it might help if they went to church together. "What's the point?" said Gloria bitterly. "Besides, you'll just be thinking about how it can help you at work." Ray was stung—partly because Gloria had a point—but he thought church was helping him with more than just work, and that Gloria had noticed. The fact that she hadn't hurt. Although the tapes had been useful, he missed being present at the service. Since it had become difficult for them to be together in the hospital room, Ray asked Gloria if she minded if he took David to church with him Sunday morning. She shrugged and said she didn't care. So they went, leaving her alone with Lindsey and the Sunday paper.

Ray was touched to see how the Sunday School kids welcomed David. They seemed genuinely glad to have him back, and David hardly looked back to say good-bye to Ray. Relieved, Ray walked to the sanctuary and slipped into one of the side pews as the music began.

Ray realized he had begun to evaluate his days and weeks according to how bad they were. It had almost become a game. *Is this the worst day of my life? Is this the worst week, or was it last week?*

This week was definitely a contender. Not only was Lindsey still in a coma, the rest of his life seemed to be unraveling. He'd alienated his best friend, his son was suffering from neglect, and now his marriage was a mess. He was making progress at work, but change took time, and this month's accounting report, though more useful, did not reflect higher profits yet. He remembered what Rev. Owens had said about Joseph last Sunday. No matter what happened to him, no matter how bad it got, Joseph kept doing what he was supposed to do. That was exactly what Ray needed to do. And Ray had really tried to do the right thing, yet nothing seemed to work.

"Today we come to the sixth message in our study," Rev. Owens began. "Please turn in your Bibles to the book of Esther." Ray had no idea who Esther was, and he didn't know where to look in the Bible. He started flipping pages, hoping it looked like he knew what he was doing, and stumbled onto the book.

"Before we get into the story," continued Rev. Owens, "let me draw your attention to some significant things about the book of Esther. First of all, the events of this book take place in Susa, the capital of western Persia. It was a huge ancient city located about 200 miles east of Babylon. The royal palace was there. Second, I want you to notice that this is the only book in the Old Testament where the name of God is not mentioned. Now don't misunderstand. God's people are in this book, and God's care for his people is clearly demonstrated here. He's just not mentioned by name.

"We need to remember that God is always with us. He may not tell us He's with us. We may not hear His voice or hear His name. But God is always with us. We're going to see this in the story of Esther."

Sure, Ray thought tiredly, *Right, but where was God this week?*

"In Esther, chapter one, the Persian King Xerxes holds a great banquet for all of his nobles, officials, and military. Everybody who is anybody is at this huge feast, which lasts for seven days. The banquet is held in an enclosed garden at the palace. Blue and white draperies hanging from silver rings, and gold and silver couches rest on floors made of marble and mother-of-pearl.

They're serving wine in goblets of gold; each one is different from the other. And the king is liberal with everything, including the wine. Verse 8 tells us that King Xerxes instructed the wine stewards to serve each man what he wished. Today we'd call it a lavish party with an open bar.

"So," he continued, "while the men are all toasting one another and drinking as much as they want, the queen is holding a banquet for all of the women. Things reach a climax on the seventh day when King Xerxes, in 'high spirits' as the Bible says in verse 10, commands his servants to go get the queen so he can parade her beauty in front of everyone. When the queen refuses, and who can blame her, the king becomes furious.

"To make a long story short, King Xerxes banishes her from his presence forever, and a search is begun for a new queen. This is where Esther enters the picture. Esther, a beautiful woman, attracts the attention of the supervisor of the king's harem. The supervisor (a sort of talent scout, I imagine) gives her beauty treatments, special food, and seven maids, then moves her to the best place of the harem, all in preparation for her presentation to the king.

"Now Esther is a Jew, but she never reveals this because her cousin Mordecai, who has raised her like a daughter, tells her not to. A year goes by. When Esther is brought to the king, everyone is impressed. Verse 17 tells us that King Xerxes is more attracted to her than anyone else, so he sets a royal crown on her head and makes her queen. He gives a great banquet in her honor, proclaims a holiday, and distributes gifts throughout the provinces.

"Meanwhile, in the court there's a wicked man named Haman who hates the Jewish people and demands their worship. Mordecai refuses to bow to him; he bows only to God, which really irritates Haman. One day Haman can't stand it any longer, so he develops a plot to do away with the Jewish people, including Mordecai. He tells King Xerxes there are people in his kingdom who have different customs and who refuse to obey his laws. Haman says it's dangerous to tolerate them, and he convinces the king to issue a decree to kill all of the Jewish people—young and old, men and women and little children—all in a single day."

Ray couldn't believe he'd never heard this story before. Action, intrigue, it was like a political thriller!

"But Mordecai finds out about the plot and sends word to Esther to warn her. He urges her to go to the king, beg him for mercy, and plead for her people. She sends word back to him. I want you to read it with me in verse 11: 'All the king's officials and the people of the royal provinces know that for any man or woman who approaches the king in the inner court without being summoned the king has but one law: that he be put to death. The only exception to this is for the king to extend the gold scepter to him and spare his life. But thirty days have passed since I was called to go to the king.'

"What a mess! Both Mordecai and Esther are in a life-or-death situation. What should they do? If they do nothing, they'll surely die. If Esther goes to the king to plead for mercy, she may be killed for entering the court uninvited.

"What would you do? Would you run? Would you try to find someone else to solve the problem? Would you ignore it and hope it would go away? Sadly, too often, too many of us do just that. And the result is that we keep living with the same problems day after day, week after week, and year after year.

"Look at what Mordecai says to Esther in chapter 4, verse 14. It's one of the best-known verses in the Bible: 'Who knows but that you have come to a royal position for such a time as this?' In other words, maybe you're the person God has placed in the right place at the right time to solve this terrible problem.

"In chapter 5, Esther goes to the king and deals with the problem head on. How does she manage to do it? I think it's because she understands our sixth principle: *The cost of solving a problem is usually less than the cost of trying to ignore one.*"

Ray wrote that down quickly. He doodled with his pen, underlining the last part of the principle when Rev. Owens drew his attention again.

"If you read the rest of Esther's story, you'll discover that not only were she and Mordecai spared, but all of the Jewish people were spared with them. What's more, Haman, the man who plotted their destruction, was hung on the very gallows he had designed and built for Mordecai. King Xerxes then issued a new decree that protected the Jewish people! And it all happened because Esther was willing to trust God, risk her own life, and take the steps necessary to solve what seemed to be an impossible problem."

After the service, Ray waited at the end of the long line of people who wanted to say a word to Rev. Owens. Several times he thought he should just leave, but something kept him there. When he finally got to the front of the line, Ray shook the pastor's hand and said, "Ray Miller." Ray wasn't sure if Rev. Owens would recognize him outside the hospital.

"Of course, Ray. How's Lindsey?" Rev. Owens seemed genuinely concerned.

"About the same," Ray answered, determined not to cry. "Your concern has meant so much to our family. But, there's something else I need to talk to you about."

"Sure, what is it?" Rev. Owens asked.

"I . . . well, I . . . uh," Ray stammered to get the words out, embarrassed.

"It's okay, Ray." Rev. Owens put his arm around Ray's shoulders just as he'd done in the hospital. It was comforting and Ray summoned up his courage.

"Gloria and I have a problem that's too costly to ignore," said Ray, trying to ignore the lump in his throat.

Rev. Owens nodded. "Would the two of you like to come in to talk about it?"

Ray had no idea what Gloria would think, but he figured her response couldn't be worse than anything else she had said to him recently.

So they agreed to meet Tuesday morning.

15

Monday morning, Ray met with John Brady to give him a crash course in ABM. John said, "Okay, Ray. You have one hour to make me smart about this. If it takes more than that, it's probably too complicated."

Ray smiled. One of John's strengths as a manager was his insistence on simplicity. It forced everyone to think clearly, and it saved a lot of time. Ray knew John would appreciate ABM for this very reason. Therefore, he was prepared to be succinct.

Ray nodded. "I think I can do it in half an hour, John. Here are copies of our traditional P&L and our new ABM P&L to help you to see what I'm going to describe. Let's start with the basics."

John spread the two P&Ls out on the table in front of him and said, "Okay, take me through it."

Megna Electronics Traditional P&L ($000s)	Actual	Budget	Variance
Sales	$35,000	$38,000	-$3,000
Cost of Goods Sold	20,000	17,000	3,000
Gross Margin	15,000	21,000	-6,000
	43%	55%	
Sales	4,000	4,100	-100
Marketing	3,000	2,900	100
Finance	2,000	2,200	-200
R & D	4,000	4,500	-500
Personnel	2,000	2,000	0
	$15,000	$15,700	-$700
	43%	41%	
Pre-Tax Profit	$0	$5,300	-$5,300
	0%	14%	

Megna Electronics ABM P&L ($000s)	Value	Non-Value	Total
Sales	$35,000	$0	$35,000
Less: Raw Materials	9,000	1,000	10,000
Less: Procurement Process	2,000	700	2,700
Sales Order Process	2,000	1,500	3,500
Manufacturing Process	6,400	2,900	9,300
New Product Process	1,500	500	2,000
Compliance Process	1,000	500	1,500
Budgeting Process	200	400	600
Maintenance Process	500	500	1,000
Marketing Process	2,000	1,500	3,500
Management Process	390	10	400
People Process	450	50	500
Total Processes	$16,440	$8,560	$25,000
TOTAL COSTS	$25,440	$9,560	$35,000
Pre-Tax Profit	$9,560	-$9,560	$0

"First, you should understand that activities consume costs. The format you will recall that we used to implement this principle was the activity accounting spreadsheet. The columns represented the activities. The rows represented cost consumed by each activity," Ray began. "Second, products, services, and customers consume activities. If you understand these two principles, you have the basic foundation for the whole project."

"Okay," said John, "so what you're saying is that there are different activities that go into, say the sale of one product. Activities might be 'procure raw material' or 'expedite orders'?"

"Exactly," said Ray. "And to make wise decisions about cutting costs, we need to understand what goes into the cost of each activity, beyond just the cost of labor. In other words, we need to manage the work, not the worker." *Like Moses*, thought Ray.

"Okay, I've got it," said John. "What else?"

"Our first step, as you remember, was to identify and quantify our activities. Kathi and her team did a great job of collecting the information and analyzing it all. They used interviews with employees and managers to understand the activities performed in each department. Then they went a step further and isolated ten specific processes, each of which included several related activities. For example, the *Procurement* process includes activities such as *Receive Material* and the like. The *Sales* process includes activities like *Process Order* and *Ship Product*. Every activity performed at Megna was assigned to a process."

Receiving Department		Receive Material	Move Material	Expedite Material	Manage Employees
Supplies	$100,000 →	$60,000	$10,000	$30,000	—
Depreciation	80,000 →	10,000	60,000	10,000	—
Overtime	50,000 →	—	—	50,000	—
Salaries	400,000 →	120,000	120,000	60,000	100,000
Space	100,000 →	30,000	30,000	15,000	25,000
All Other	50,000 →	15,000	15,000	7,500	12,500
Total	$780,000	$235,000	$235,000	$172,500	$137,500
Output Measures		4,000 #of Receipts	1,620 #of Moves	860 #of Expedites	10 #of Employees
Cost per Output		$58	$145	$200	$13,750

Procurement Process

	Value	Non-Value	Total	Output Quantity	Cost per Output
Run MRP	$805,000	$0	$805,000	100	$8,050.00
Issue P.O.	800,000	0	800,000	16,000	$50.00
Expedite P.O.	0	400,000	400,000	4,000	$100.00
Receive Material	235,000	0	235,000	4,000	$58.75
Inspect Material	0	250,000	250,000	560	$446.42
Certify Supplier	60,000	0	60,000	20	$3,000.00
Pay Invoice	100,000	50,000	150,000	8,000	$18.75
	$2,000,000	$700,000	$2,700,000		
	75%	25%	42,100 parts		
			$64.13 per part		

Megna Electronics ABC P&L ($000s)	Value	Non-Value	Total
Sales	$35,000	$0	$35,000
Less: Raw Materials	9,000	1,000	10,000
Less: Procurement Process	2,000	700	2,700
Sales Order Process	2,000	1,500	3,500
Manufacturing Process	6,400	2,900	9,300
New Product Process	1,500	500	2,000
Compliance Process	1,000	500	1,500
Budgeting Process	200	400	600
Maintenance Process	500	500	1,000
Marketing Process	2,000	1,500	3,500
Management Process	390	10	400
People Process	450	50	500
Total Processes	$16,440	$8,560	$25,000
TOTAL COSTS	$25,440	$9,560	$35,000
Pre-Tax Profit	$9,560	-$9,560	$0

John studied the P&L as Ray went on. "We knew we'd be doing ourselves a favor if we kept our customers happy." *Thank God for Rahab,* Ray thought. Aloud he said, "Megna prospers when its customers are happy, and we need to do the same in the accounting department. All the managers are our internal customers, so we need to find a way to make our information useful to them." It was hard for Ray to believe that it had only been four weeks since the meeting when everyone seemed to have had permission to bash the accountants. So much had happened since then.

John asked, "So, have you found a way?"

Ray nodded. "We're getting there. Identifying processes helped. The team's next step was to talk to employees about waste—in other words, activities that are the result of mistakes and that don't contribute to the bottom line in any way. That's when they began categorizing specific tasks as *value* or *non-value* activities. And that's information that can really help the managers. They can take a look at the *non-value* activities and find opportunities to save money.

"But that's when we ran into a snag and called you in for help. The employees think saving money means layoffs, so they don't want to cooperate. We need you to reassure them that's not what we have in mind. We need the employees to cooperate with Kathi's team by giving them information and ideas for reducing waste. I can't tell you how important it is to have your support."

John nodded. "So what else do I need to know?"

"Well," said Ray, "when you talk to the employees, your vision for the company can help them to understand that if Megna is to survive, we all need to work together. 'Us versus them' had better mean 'all of us versus the competition' and not 'workers versus managers' or any other form of internal strife.

"I know the managers understand this—it's one reason why the project has run relatively smoothly so far. The ABM team includes managers from departments with conflicting agendas, but ABM has given them a common language and common objectives. It would have been a lot harder if they had clung to their little fiefdoms and attacked each other, but they haven't." Ray gave a mental nod to David. "On the other hand, they have been willing to use other tools and resources to help our effort, things like total quality management. I give them a lot of credit for what they've accomplished so far."

"Interesting," said John. "I'm glad to hear you're not excluding other resources. What I hear you saying is that the money we've invested in tools like TQM isn't a waste, and that you are using them along with ABM. But besides infighting, what other dangers do we need to avoid?"

"Old habits," said Ray. "We all have to be willing to change." Ray's voice caught for a moment as he thought of Jonah and then Lindsey, but he cleared his throat and went on. "It would be crazy to think that we can continue using last year's unsuccessful methods and expect improved results this year. So we're working on an idea-generation program that will encourage employees to submit ideas for saving costs on a regular basis. Then we have to be willing to implement the best ideas and look for results. It sounds easy, but getting people to change is harder than you might think."

"I know," said John. "Go on."

"Changing old habits frees us up to find new ways to use our resources. For example, wasted resources can be shifted from a non-value activity to an activity that makes a positive contribution. It's a matter of consciously deciding to do the right thing all the time." Ray pictured Joseph helping his brothers. "And ABM helps us to know what the right things are. If you think about it, it's actually better to perform a profitable activity poorly than to perform an unprofitable activity extremely well. ABM helps us know what's profitable and what's not, and of course our goal is to perform only profitable activities extremely well." As Ray laid it all out for John, he understood more than ever just how right ABM was for the company.

"So that's where we are now, John. We have identified six waste-reduction options, and now we need approval to implement them. I was hoping we could take care of that at the management meeting this afternoon."

"Fine," said John. "I'll look forward to hearing the ideas. This helps, Ray. At least I feel like I can speak to the employees about it. And I get the sense that your process can teach us a lot about what Megna is doing wrong. I'd be interested to know your general observations about our operation so far—nothing formal, just an overview of your initial impressions. Could you jot them down and give them to me at the meeting this afternoon?"

"Sure," said Ray. "I'll start now."

Back in his office, Ray made a list of what he thought were the most interesting findings of the project so far. He wrote:

1. *Megna repeats mistakes.* Many of the non-value-added activities result directly from errors that are repeated daily.
2. *Work is duplicated.* Activity analysis shows that several different departments perform the same activities.
3. *Good ideas are not shared.* Organizing Megna by department instead of by process tends to isolate improvement ideas in single functions.
4. *Megna Electronics competes on price even when it's unprofitable.* ABM customer profitability analysis shows that we should tell customers, "We'll drop our price if you'll drop your demand for some activities."
5. *Megna relies too much on a few individuals.* ABM is beginning to

show us that it empowers every employee to become involved in the business. Spreadsheet-style reports make ABM more understandable to non-financial employees.

After he finished the list, Ray went to Kathi's desk. "I need your help at one o'clock. Are you free?"

"Well, yes and no. Yes, I am available at one but I won't come free. You've got to buy me lunch."

"It's a deal. John and his staff can meet with us to review the cost-reduction ideas at 1:00 p.m. Since you've done most of the work, I'd like to have you there."

"Sure. But you've provided most of the ideas. You came up with the whole idea of ABM."

"No, I didn't invent it. I just found it."

"Right," said Kathi. "Found it where?" She expected the answer to be a book, or maybe a professor or a consultant.

"You'll probably think I'm nuts, but I picked up the first basic principle at church."

"No kidding?" said Kathi. "That would be the last place I'd look for a solution to a business problem."

"Same here," said Ray. "It just sort of happened."

At lunch Ray told Kathi about the six principles he had learned so far. She listened attentively, and Ray was relieved to finally tell someone who understood. His wife knew that Rev. Owens's sermons were helping him at work, but she wasn't aware of the significance each principle had . . . their business applications. "You know, I'm glad you told me, Ray," said Kathi. "It helps me to know where you're coming from, and it's not all that weird. I'll bet lots of people learn stuff from the Bible but just don't talk about it. Maybe I'll have to check out Rev. Owens one of these days. His principles might help me with my kids."

Kathi told Ray about what it was like to bring up two sons on her own. Her teenager in particular was giving her a hard time. Nothing terrible, just a sassy attitude and laziness about chores. But the responsibility of bringing the boys up right weighed heavily on her. It was Ray's turn to listen, and he was ashamed he had never taken the time before to even think about Kathi's situation. *Everyone has problems,* he thought, *it's just that my own seem bigger.* Lindsey's condition had become a familiar ache. He wasn't learning to ignore it, but he was learning to live with it.

As they walked back to Ray's office to pick up his materials for the meeting, Ray thought about how nice it had been to have lunch with Kathi. She understood him, she liked him, she made him feel good about himself. He could forget about the mess at home when he was with her. Guiltily, Ray tried to shake these thoughts away as he headed to the conference room.

"Come on in, Ray, Kathi," said John. All the managers were sitting in their usual places around the table.

"You all know Kathi Edwards, our cost accounting manager," said Ray. "I've asked her to join us today because, as team leader for the ABM Project, she's the best person to answer your questions."

Ray turned on the overhead projector and went through the ABM findings slide by slide. He showed examples of activity accounting spreadsheets to demonstrate the data gathering process. There were just a few perfunctory questions, which Kathi easily answered. Then Ray showed some business process reports. This time there were no questions. By the time he contrasted the traditional P&L with the ABM P&L, both Ray and Kathi sensed that something was wrong. It was as if they were presenting to an iceberg.

Finally Chuck Anderson spoke up. "Ray," he said, leaning back in his chair, "everything you're showing us is interesting, but I question the validity of the data-gathering process. It seems haphazard."

"What do you mean?" asked Kathi.

"Well, for example," said Chuck, "you and Ray told us that during the departmental interviews you asked employees, 'What do you do?' and also for their best guesses about how much time and resource they spend on each activity. That doesn't sound very precise to me. We have some critical decisions to make for this company, and I just don't feel comfortable with the methods you've used. Does anyone else feel the same way?"

Dick Conway from Engineering and Mark Paley from Materials Management both said "yes" almost at the same time.

Ray jumped in before things started going downhill. "Let me see if I can explain our method with an illustration. Chuck, if you asked me to describe an acre of land, my traditional accounting response would be that an acre of land is equal to 43,560 square feet. My ABM answer would be that an acre of land is about the size of a football field without end zones. Which answer can you best understand and picture in your mind?"

"The ABM answer, of course, but I don't see what it proves," said Chuck.

"The point," said Ray, trying not to sound defensive, "is that the 43,560 square feet answer is precisely useless. The football field answer is approximately relevant. If I remember correctly, you voiced some serious concerns about our traditional cost system. In fact, I remember distinctly your using the terms 'precisely useless' and 'approximately relevant.'"

Chuck reddened. "I stand corrected. But don't get me wrong. I think the ABM information does give us a useful perspective. The activity, process, and value information you guys have uncovered is terrific. I guess my concern is that we are relying upon employees to tell us what they do and where they spend their time. Doesn't that seem a little risky?"

"That's really an issue of trust," Ray explained. "If you want to go down to Order Processing and tell those ladies they don't know what they're doing, or what adds value and what doesn't, then be my guest."

Chris, who manages Order Processing, laughed and said, "Chuck, you're welcome to go down there, but I advise you to put on your bulletproof vest. They'll jump all over you if you try to tell them they don't know their business. They know it a lot better than we do."

"Okay, okay, guys," John said, "I appreciate your concerns, but I think we can agree that if we spend our time making the ABM analysis more precise, we won't arrive at a significantly different answer. Let's go with what we've got. Ray, Kathi, what's our next step?"

Ray said, "There are three things to discuss before we leave today. First, we need to agree on what to do with excess resources that are freed up as a result of improving activities or business processes." Ray put up an overhead displaying the six options he had developed for dealing with waste:

- Fund growth of value activities in the same department
- Fund growth of value activities in other departments
- Fund totally new activities
- Redirect resources to departments that can increase sales revenue
- Eliminate through attrition
- Eliminate immediately (e.g., layoff, curtailed budget, etc.)

Everyone agreed with the options and also the order of priority shown by the list.

"Next, I've asked John to meet with all the employees in small groups to accomplish three things: to motivate them to cooperate with the ABM team, to dispel rumors that we're planning layoffs, and to build their trust by giving them the facts. First, he's going to talk about the importance of continuous improvement for Megna Electronics and why we need their continued participation in ABM workshops. Second, he has the six waste options to show them that layoffs are the last thing we would do. And third, he'll be up front and answer their questions."

"I definitely think this is the right thing to do," said John. "All I ask is that you or Kathi be with me at every meeting in case there's a technical question regarding ABM."

"No problem," said Ray.

"So what's the third issue, Ray?" said John.

"I need each of you to go back to your department managers and stress that the messenger of bad news will not be shot."

"Can you explain, Ray?" said Mary Forsman.

"We don't want people to be afraid to report a problem. They need to know they're not going to be fired or get a bad review or end up in the mailroom. If we are going to make this company the best it can be, we need every employee to know that we want their input, that we need their input, and that we will use their input. We want them to know that it's better to solve a problem than to ignore one, even if it seems risky. So, no shooting the messenger. Got it?"

"Geez, Ray, we get it already," said Chuck.

"Ray makes a good point, though," said Mary. "From what I've seen, I'm convinced that not only can we meet headquarters' profit goals, we can exceed them. But we need everyone's input. We can't afford fear right now."

"I agree," said John. "As I see it, now comes the hard part. We have to put it all into action."

16

Ray and Gloria met with Rev. Owens for over two hours on Tuesday morning. Ray had given Gloria the tape of the last sermon and asked her to listen to it Monday evening while he and David went out for burgers. What he didn't know was that she had spent most of the past week asking God to help save her marriage and her family.

Gloria listened to the tape. When he returned, Ray apologized for what he had recently said and done. Ray told Gloria how important she was to him, how he knew that the cost of ignoring their problems was far greater than the cost of facing them, and how he'd taken a risk and talked to Rev. Owens. At first Gloria was thrown by the loss of privacy. She knew Ray was right but hated the idea of unveiling their problems to someone else. But since Ray had taken the first step to make things right, and apologized, she agreed to meet with Rev. Owens to discuss their marriage.

Rev. Owens's office looked like it was made of books. Books seemed to hold up the walls and support his desk. And not just religious books either. There were biographies of American presidents, collections of essays by the world's great thinkers, volumes on art and music, even contemporary novels. Ray's surprise at the pastor's library revealed to him that he had unconsciously pegged most religious believers as narrow-minded and uneducated. But Rev. Owens had obviously read widely, and his faith had apparently withstood intellectual scrutiny.

Two hours passed like the blink of an eye. Ray and Gloria

made good progress too. They even laughed several times, which surprised all three of them, in light of what they'd been discussing.

Rev. Owens explained that Lindsey's accident had only exacerbated some problems that already existed in their family, problems they needed to work on. But he also told them that some of the problems were a direct result of the accident, like Ray's argument with Bill over suing the delivery company and David's problems at school, for example. He even suggested that given the stress of the past few weeks, they should be thankful things were no worse than they were.

They talked through each problem and how to deal with it. After two hours, Rev. Owens's secretary came in looking concerned and said, "I'm sorry to interrupt, but the hospital just left a message for Mr. and Mrs. Miller. They need you to come to the hospital right away. You are to go to the doctor's lounge."

Ray and Gloria didn't need any more details. They knew this was it; their worst fears had come true.

The Millers ran out of the church building and jumped into the car. Ray drove under the speed limit this time; it was almost as if he wanted to delay hearing the news—it could be the worst words of his life. Neither of them spoke as Ray pulled into a parking space. They entered the hospital and headed to the elevators. Once inside, Ray pushed the button for floor two on the elevator panel. Gloria slipped her hand into his, squeezing hard.

The doors opened on the second floor and they looked for the sign to the doctor's lounge. Holding hands, they walked down the carpeted hallway to the door with the DOCTOR'S LOUNGE sign. They poked their head in and saw Dr. Cochran writing something on a chart. He closed the folder, smiled tentatively and said, "Please come in and sit down."

Ray thought angrily, *This is no time to encourage me with a smile. Just give it to me straight.*

The doctor removed his glasses, began to wipe them, and said simply, "She's awake."

There was a knock at the door and Rev. Owens joined them.

"I'm sorry," said Ray. "I didn't hear what you said."

"Lindsey woke up," said the doctor.

"What?" Gloria said, not fully comprehending. "Where is she?"

Ray's heart was pounding; he found he had no voice.

"She came out of the coma just a few minutes before we called," the doctor said, grinning.

"She's alive!" Gloria shouted as she threw her arms around Ray. They both cried and laughed and cried some more.

"Oh, my God," said Ray. He pumped the doctor's hand and hugged Rev. Owens. "She's alive! She made it!"

"Can we see her?" said Gloria.

"Absolutely, and she wants to see you," said the doctor. "We don't know what happened or why. There's no medical or scientific explanation for it. After three weeks in a coma, she just woke up. So we want to be careful and not overtax her. After you've spent a little time with her, we need to set up a rehab program for her. We don't know how much damage she's sustained, or even if there is any. We'll begin some tests early this afternoon that will give us a better idea. But what you need to know is that, even though she's awake, we'll need to keep her here for a while just to make sure she's all right and ready to go home. Okay?"

"Sure," said Ray.

"Thank you!" Gloria wept as she hugged the doctor and said, "Thank you! Thank you! Thank you!"

"I've got to make a couple of stops," said the doctor, "so I'll meet you in Lindsey's room in a few minutes." Then he left the three of them alone.

Ray turned to Rev. Owens and said, "Would you say a few words of thanks with us?"

Rev. Owens smiled. "I can't think of anything I'd rather do right now." And there in the doctor's lounge the three of them gave thanks for the miracle of Lindsey's life.

Lindsey was sitting up in her bed when they walked in. "Hey!" she said.

And then they were a jumble of kisses and hugs and tears and "I love you's."

"Honey, do you remember Rev. Owens from church? He's helped us a lot while you've been sick."

"Nice to meet you," said Lindsey. "Mom, I'm starving. Is there anything to eat?"

"Those are the best words I've heard all month," said Gloria. "Let me go see what I can find."

The doctors allowed Lindsey to have some Jell-O before beginning a battery of tests. That afternoon, while Lindsey was being pricked and prodded, Gloria used up an entire phone card at the pay phone calling relatives and friends to tell them the good news. Ray called his secretary and asked her to tell everyone at Megna.

Later Gloria went home to get some things Lindsey wanted: extra clothes, tapes for her Walkman, and her favorite pillow. Lindsey asked to see David too. These were all signs that she was on the road to recovery, and Ray savored every one of them.

Ray and Gloria stayed outside but listened at the door when David went in to see Lindsey for the first time. They weren't sure what to expect. At first there was silence. Ray fought the urge to go in and break the ice. But then he heard David telling Lindsey about a frog he had found in Sandy's backyard and about the Simpsons' episodes she had missed. Before long they were laughing and goofing around as if nothing had happened. Ray felt like an idiot. It hadn't even occurred to him that David had missed Lindsey.

The number of visitors increased during the next week with relatives, neighbors, and friends from school dropping by. Lindsey's room looked like a birthday party gone wild. Flowers, cards, balloons, and stuffed animals filled every inch of space.

The tests revealed nothing abnormal as far as anyone could tell. The physical therapists had done a good job of exercising Lindsey's arms and legs while she was still in the coma. Despite four weeks in bed, she was in reasonably good shape. There was some tingling in her fingers and toes, and she felt a little lightheaded whenever she sat up, but she was able to take a few steps with a walker each morning and afternoon. Slowly but surely it was all coming back to her.

While Lindsey was in therapy Sunday morning, Gloria, Ray, and David went to church. When they walked into the sanctuary, things seemed different. People they'd never met before acted as if they knew them and congratulated them on Lindsey's recovery. It took Ray and Gloria a few minutes to figure it out. These people had been praying for their family all along! David sat with them instead of going to children's church; today he wanted to be with his mom and dad.

The whole service seemed more meaningful to them this morning. The music sounded fuller. The words to the songs seemed to be about them. Ray put a large check in the offering plate. When Gloria looked at it and then at him, he shrugged and whispered, "It seems so little compared to what we've been given."

Then Rev. Owens came to the pulpit to preach. He looked out over the crowd, saw Ray, and smiled. "Please turn in your Bibles to Judges, chapter 13," he said. "Today we meet a man named Samson. Samson has been called the Bible's he-man with a she-weakness." The congregation laughed. "He is famous for his incredible feats of strength. But he's also known for his incredible weakness when it came to Philistine women.

"Before Samson was born, an angel appeared to his mother and told her she would have a son. This came as quite a shock; she was childless and believed she was sterile. The angel warned her not to drink wine or eat unclean food during her pregnancy. Note that this was long before medical science had discovered the dangers of alcohol and unhealthy food to an unborn baby, but God knows everything. He always has and He always will.

"Anyway, Samson's mother was also told never to cut his hair, because he was to be a Nazirite, that is, a person who took a vow to be set apart for God's service. As a Nazirite, Samson could not cut his hair, touch a dead body, or drink anything containing alcohol. For some, the Nazirite vow was only temporary, but Samson was to be a Nazirite all his life. And God was going to use him to set in motion Israel's deliverance from the Philistines.

"Chapter 14 tells us that when Samson was a young man, he fell in love with a young Philistine woman and asked his parents to make the marriage arrangements. Although the Philistines were Israel's worst enemy, Samson and his parents went to meet her. On the way, the Bible says, a lion came roaring toward him. But as it did, the Spirit of the Lord came upon Samson, giving him supernatural strength, and he tore the lion apart with his bare hands."

"Cool," whispered David. Ray and Gloria rolled their eyes.

"Later Samson challenged some of the guests at his wedding feast to solve a riddle. He bet them thirty sets of clothes and linen garments each if they could solve it. They were stumped, so they made Samson's wife find out the answer by threatening her. She begged Samson, sobbing, until he told her. Then she gave away the answer.

"When his guests answered correctly, Samson knew he had been tricked. Again, the Spirit of the Lord got him out of a tight situation. God gave him the power to overcome thirty Philistine men in another town. Samson took their clothes and paid off his bet.

"Then Samson caught three hundred foxes. He tied their tails together and fastened a torch to every two tails. He lit the torches and let the foxes loose in the Philistines' grain fields. Everything burned up—the fields and groves of the Philistines and also their vineyards. In retribution, the Philistines burned Samson's wife and her father to death. Samson retaliated by slaughtering many of them. He then hid in a cave. Finally, Samson allowed himself to be captured and handed over to the Philistines. He agreed to let them tie him up. But once again, the Spirit of the Lord gave him the power to snap the ropes. He killed a thousand Philistines with the jawbone of a donkey."

David was on the edge of his seat.

"Another time, in Gaza, while Samson spent the night with a prostitute, the people gathered at the city gates, plotting to capture and kill him. Instead, Samson got up in the middle of the night, and with the power given to him by the Spirit of the Lord, he took the gates of the city and carried them off to the top of a hill!

"Do you see a pattern here? Samson is set apart for God's service and is given incredible power by the Spirit of the Lord. Samson keeps getting himself into scrapes, and his God-given strength gives him a way out. You'd think he would learn not to get into these scrapes. What a waste of his God-given power!

"Well, then Samson falls in love with another Philistine woman, Delilah. You've probably heard of her, and also how she brought about Samson's demise. Actually, Samson was his own worst enemy. He became responsible for his own death because he thought he could keep doing the same thing over and over and expect the same results. The rulers of the Philistines bribed Delilah to find out the secret to Samson's strength so they could overpower him.

"So Delilah nagged him until he gave in. Samson told her that as a Nazirite he had been given special power by God. If his hair were cut, he would no longer have that power. Chapter 16, verse 20 relates the devastating details. Delilah cut his hair as he slept, then called out: 'Samson, the Philistines are upon you!' Samson woke up and thought, 'I'll go out as before and shake myself free.' But he doesn't know that the Lord's power had left him.

"It's tragic. The Philistines capture him, gouge out his eyes, bind him with shackles, and place him in a prison grinding grain. Now, I don't want you to miss this. Samson illustrates for us one of the most important principles we'll learn in this series. Principle Number Seven: *You can't do the same thing over and over again and expect better results.* You've got to keep growing, maturing, and improving, learning from your mistakes *and* your successes."

Ray summarized the thought and wrote it down: *You can't do the same thing over and over again expecting better results. You've got to keep growing, maturing, and improving.*

"Samson thought success was just a matter of doing the same thing over and over again. But that's not success, that's insanity. Especially if you're expecting better results. Samson's mistake was relying on his previous successes. He kept thinking, 'I can do it again. No problem. It worked before, it'll work again.' The tragic, unnecessary end of his life demonstrates for us the folly of this philosophy.

"Let me ask you a question. How many people do you know who live their lives like Samson? Are they content to coast, choosing to try to go through life on cruise control? You can't drive a car like that for very long and you can't live your life like that either. You have to keep growing. You have to keep maturing. You've got to commit yourself to improving every day."

Ray looked at the notes he'd made on his card. He thought,

"Things can't be like they were before Lindsey's accident—they have to get better. We can't just go back to the way things were. No same old, same old. We have to make our suffering worth something. We must learn from it and improve." He wrote the word "IMPROVE" in capital letters and underlined it several times. Then he wrote: "no coasting."

17

Driving to work Monday, Ray thought about Rev. Owens's sermon about Samson and Principle Seven: *You can't do the same thing over and over again and expect better results.* "The problem with life, is not that it's one thing after another. The problem is that we do the same things over and over as different things come up. Implementing ABM will make us do things differently, and it will show us what activities not to repeat. It certainly makes us look at things differently."

Ray was a little disappointed though. He had been so struck by the principle's application to his personal life, that he had expected it to give him some dramatic insight into Megna's situation too. But other than making him more vigilant about slipping into old habits and old patterns of thinking, Ray couldn't see how else it applied.

He pulled into the parking lot at the same time as John, so they walked into the building together. John slapped Ray on the back and said, "Great news about Lindsey, Ray. I can't even imagine how hard these weeks have been for you, and with overhauling the accounting system here on top of it all!"

Ray smiled. "Thanks. Actually, in a way, the ABM project has helped keep me sane." He explained. "It gave me something else to think about besides Lindsey's accident. I would have been a screaming lunatic if I'd had nothing else in my head. There was nothing I could do for her, so I was glad to be doing something here at least." Saying this out loud made Ray understand a little better why Gloria had started to fall apart last week, and he shuddered at his own insensitivity.

"Well, you're doing a great job, Ray. But we need to see some tangible results soon."

"I know," said Ray. "Kathi tells me that everyone has been more cooperative since you had your talks with the employees. I can't tell you enough what a difference it made to have leadership and support from top management, and from you personally."

"I'm glad it worked out," said John as he went into his office.

Kathi came by to congratulate Ray on Lindsey's recovery and to brief him on some of the employees' cost reduction ideas.

"I'll bet you can't wait to have your family back to normal. When does she get to come home?" she asked.

"It'll be a couple of weeks yet," said Ray, "but she's making progress every day."

"Well," said Kathi, "we're making progress every day here. I've really enjoyed this project, Ray, but I have to admit that once we fix Megna's problems, I'm anxious to have everything back to normal again too."

Ray shook his head. "I hate to disappoint you, Kathi, but we're never going back to normal. Don't you remember? Normal was the problem. You're the one who wanted to throw away the old cost accounting commandments."

"I know," said Kathi, "but don't you think that now that we have a new system it will run fairly automatically, once we work out the kinks? I mean, we're not going to perpetually reinvent the wheel, are we?"

"No," said Ray, "but we have to continually improve the wheel. When we coast, we're going downhill. And I'm afraid that if we coast too long on the same wheel, we'll eventually wear it out. And then we won't be able to keep up with the folks who have better wheels."

"So you're saying we can't afford to get tired," said Kathi, laughing at her own pun.

Ray rolled his eyes. "No, as a matter of fact we can't. ABM isn't a diet of whittle your 'waste' in thirty days and that's it. It's a process of ongoing improvement."

"Ongoing, like *forever?*" asked Kathi, her eyes widening.

"I think so," said Ray. "We won't always be going through the dramatic changes we're in right now, but I do think we'll have to keep getting better all the time. You know, when Lindsey was lying unconscious for so long, all I wanted was for that little girl to be alive. Just like right now, and how what we want most is for Megna to make its numbers, right? But now that Lindsey's awake, I realize that's not enough. I want her to be healthy and strong, to walk without a walker. And after that, I want her to keep growing and to become, well it sounds corny, but to become the best she can be. To fulfill her potential as an adult.

"So, sure," Ray continued, "the first thing is for Megna to get on its feet. And that's the most dramatic thing we're hoping to do here. But then we'll need to keep analyzing our costs and making changes. Otherwise we'll become just as stagnant and as set in our ways as before. You can't keep doing the same things over and over and expect improved results."

"That sounds like another principle," said Kathi.

Ray winked and said, "Samson."

After Kathi left, Ray thought about the principle some more. He realized that it wasn't as simple as he had thought. It wasn't only about leaving the old behind. It was also about not letting the new get old. Megna couldn't afford to simply adopt a new system and then "get back to normal." Ray had been so excited about how much better **ABM** was than the old system that he had not even thought about how much better the new system could become. So it wasn't just about meeting the year's projections—it was about exceeding them, and then putting Megna on the path to ever-increasing profitability. ABM wasn't just a short-term fix; it was a way to long-term growth.

The challenge was to put the principles into practice. How could they possibly do it in time? And this was a short week with Thursday and Friday off for Thanksgiving.

18

Lindsey continued to improve. The doctors were amazed at her daily progress. They told Ray and Gloria that if she continued to improve at the same rate, she might be able to go home in the next week! Ray and Gloria were thrilled, but they didn't want to get Lindsey's hopes up until they knew for sure.

Since Lindsey's recovery, David's behavior had changed at school. His visits with Lindsey each afternoon were a special treat. He stayed out of trouble so he wouldn't have to stay in detention after school. And Ray made a point of spending time alone with David each day, even if only for a few minutes.

With Lindsey recovering and David back in line, things had also improved between Ray and Gloria. They had begun to relax a little and were enjoying each other's company again. There were still difficulties to work through, but nothing seemed impossible now. And there was so much to be thankful for.

They had a makeshift Thanksgiving dinner in Lindsey's room. Ray picked up some turkey dinners at the local Boston Market, and Sandy brought by a pumpkin pie. They ate with their plates on their laps; it was really more of a Thanksgiving picnic. But it was the best Thanksgiving the family had ever had, and it would forever hold a special place in their memories.

Ray went into the office on Friday to get some more work done while the phones weren't ringing. Gloria and David stayed and played board games with Lindsey. Saturday was Ray's turn in the hospital while Gloria took David to a movie for some quality time.

A Sunday morning routine had been established. The Millers went to church while Lindsey went to her morning therapy. Ray had his note cards ready in the pew, and he smiled when he saw Gloria pull some blank cards out of her purse.

Rev. Owens began as usual with a prayer. Ray had never paid much attention to what he thought of as Rev. Owens's "warm-up" prayer. This time, however, he listened as Rev. Owens said, "Father, speak through me this morning, and open our hearts and our minds so that we might learn from You just what we need to know today, wherever we are in our tired lives. Amen."

"Interesting," thought Ray. He had assumed it was Rev. Owens who was teaching him the principles. But the prayer suggested the pastor was just the messenger.

Rev. Owens looked out at the congregation as he began, "Please turn with me now to the book of Numbers, where we meet the eighth Bible character in our series."

Gloria leaned over and whispered, "You should like this, you're a numbers guy." Ray groaned.

"So far," said Rev. Owens, "we have learned seven great life-changing principles that can help all of us, in our families, our businesses, any place and at any time. These principles can help us succeed. But only if we apply them do we get results.

"The Bible makes an interesting statement about the man we're going to meet. This is God speaking in Numbers, chapter 14: 'But because my servant Caleb has a different spirit and follows me wholeheartedly, I will bring him into the land he went to, and his descendants will inherit it.'"

Rev. Owens went on. "Ladies and gentlemen, meet Caleb, our eighth Bible character. God says he 'had a different spirit' and followed Him 'wholeheartedly.' That would be enough to merit our respect and attention this morning. But listen to the rest of the story.

"The story takes place when God brings the people of Israel to the edge of the Promised Land. He promised to give them this land. But before they move in, Moses sent twelve men to check it out. Among them are Caleb and also Joshua, whom you'll remember from the story of Rahab. In chapter 13, these spies come back to Moses and give their report. 'We went into the land to which you sent us, and it does flow with milk and honey! Here is its fruit. But the people who live there are powerful, and the cities are fortified and very large.'

"Then Caleb stood up and said, 'We should go up and take possession of the land for we can certainly do it.' But the others speak against him. 'We can't attack those people; they are stronger than we are.' And they spread among the Israelites a bad report about the land they had explored. 'The land we explored devours those living in it. All the people we saw there are of great size. . . . We seemed like grasshoppers in our own eyes, and we looked the same to them.'

"Now, get the picture. God has promised this land to His people. Moses sends men in to check it out. They come back, and ten out of twelve of them say, 'We can't do it.'

"Caleb, on the other hand, was confident of God's promise. 'We can do it!' Remember, he had a 'different spirit.' His response also illustrates the eighth principle: *When you make wrong comparisons you always come up with wrong conclusions.* The mistake the ten other spies made was this: They made faulty comparisons and came up with a foolish conclusion.

"Caleb made the right comparison and came up with the right conclusion. The negative spies said, 'We're like grasshoppers compared to these giants.' But Caleb, supported by Joshua, says in chapter 14, verse 9, 'Do not be afraid of the people in the land, because we will swallow them up. Their protection is gone, but the Lord is with us. Do not be afraid of them.' In other words, when compared to *God*, the *giants* are like grasshoppers.

"Why were their perspectives so completely different? Because Caleb had a 'different spirit' and he 'followed the Lord wholeheartedly.' This enabled him to make the right comparisons—and, ultimately, helped him come to the right conclusions. The result? God rewarded Caleb's faith and Joshua's too. He let Caleb and Joshua actually enter the Promised Land. None of the others ever got there."

Ray had been taking notes throughout the message, and Gloria had taken notes too. She'd written: "Compared to God, no problem is too big." Ray looked at her and nodded, then pointed to his notes. Toward the bottom of his card, Ray had written: "Wrong comparison = wrong conclusions = wrong results." He underlined results, remembering what John Brady had said.

In the car after the service, Ray and Gloria discussed the message. Ray said, "Honey, do you know how many times over the past few weeks I thought to myself, 'Why us? Why our family?'" I even wondered, "Why couldn't we be like our neighbors, who never seem to have problems?"

"I know. I did the same thing." Gloria said. "But then, when I compared ourselves with the people I met in the ICU waiting room that first week, people whose loved ones died, we seemed a lot better off."

"Same here," said Ray. "Have you ever paid much attention to what Rev. Owens says when he prays at the beginning?"

"Not really, why?"

"Well, I hadn't realized it, but all along I've actually thought Rev. Owens was the source of the wisdom we've been getting in church. Today it occurred to me that he is a very gifted speaker and has an unusual ability to pull practical lessons out of these stories, but he's just the translator of the message, not the author himself."

"So who's the author?" asked Gloria. Ray could tell she was thinking. Then Gloria said quietly, "Oh, I get it. I never thought about that either."

19

Ray ran into Chris Meyers as he walked down the hallway to the cafeteria.

"How's it going, Ray?" said Chris.

"Terrific, but I'm improving!" said Ray.

"Hey, we could use you in Sales with an attitude like that," said Chris.

"No thanks," said Ray. "I've got my hands full in finance. Nice tie." The tie was dark blue with tiny fir trees woven in an intricate design.

"It's that time of year," said Chris. "Got time for a joke?"

"Sure," said Ray. "Why not?"

Chris grinned like a kid. "Okay, so there's this large dog that walks into a butcher shop carrying a purse in his mouth. He puts the purse down and sits in front of the meat case. 'What is it, boy?' the butcher asks, joking. 'Want to buy some meat?' The dog barks. 'Hmm,' says the butcher. 'What kind? Liver, bacon, steak ...?' 'Woof!' says the dog. 'Okay, how much steak?' says the butcher. 'Half a pound, one pound ...?' 'Woof!' says the dog. The butcher nods and wraps up a pound of meat. Sure enough, he finds money in the dog's purse. He's amazed by all this, so when the dog leaves, he follows. The dog enters an apartment building, climbs to the third floor, and begins scratching at a door. The door swings open and an angry man starts shouting at the dog. 'Stop!' yells the butcher. 'Why are you yelling at this dog? He's the most intelligent animal I've ever seen!' 'Intelligent?' says the man. 'This is the third time this week he's forgotten his key.'"

Ray laughed. "You don't know how much that story hits home."

"What do you mean?" asked Chris.

"Well, it seems to me that some of the people here are like the butcher. They're amazed when they see ABM for the first time. Others are like the dog's owner. They say, 'What's the big deal? We've seen it before.' They've seen other business improvement methods with three-letter names come and go at Megna. They're skeptical. 'Why would ABM be any different?' or so they think."

"Well, you've won me over," said Chris.

"How do you mean?"

"You know that customer profitability analysis that Kathi prepared? Well, I sat down the other day with the purchasing manager at Greenbelt Computer and showed him the activity portion. Then I told him that if he would agree to change his buying pattern with us, I'd reduce his price."

"What?" asked Ray.

"I showed him how much it costs for us to process a standard order, an expedite, and a change order. I told him we couldn't reduce his sales price unless he placed orders monthly instead of weekly. Then I told him we would gladly expedite his orders or change them, but that, given the lower price, we would have to charge him a service fee. He thought about it for fifteen seconds and then agreed."

"Why do you think he agreed?"

"Well, for one thing," said Chris, "his boss measures his performance on purchase price. If I lower his prices on Megna parts, he'll be a hero. At least for a day or two."

"I can understand that, but why would he agree to a service charge for expedites or change orders?" asked Ray.

"Two reasons. First, there was never a consequence or penalty for expediting in the past. Expedites were free. Now he'll think twice before changing his order or requesting an expedite. Second, he can pass our expedite fee on to the customers who made the request. He'll probably take our fee and mark it up for a profit," said Chris.

"Makes sense to me," said Ray.

"Me too," said Chris. "I can't wait to roll out ABC menu-based pricing to all our customers. How soon will we be able to do it?"

"I don't know off the top of my head," said Ray. "I'll have to check with Kathi and Dick. But we'll get it done for you. That's great news. ABM not only helped us keep a customer, but it will likely generate more revenue and reduce costs for us at the same time."

"Sounds good," said Chris.

"Make sure you tell John about this," Ray suggested. He didn't want to be the only one bragging about ABM to the boss.

"I'll talk to him later today," Chris promised as he began to walk up the stairs to his office. "When will you have a timetable for the ABM rollout?"

"I'm not sure, but I'll let you know on Friday."

"Great," said Chris, "and you owe me a joke."

When Ray returned to his office, he thought about his conversation with Chris. *Chris is actually excited about this new costing system,* he thought. *How could we have spent so many years measuring the wrong things? Who knows how many performance measures, or other aspects of the accounting system, need to be changed?*

Ray opened his briefcase and pulled out the note he had written at the end of Rev. Owens's sermon. It said, Wrong Comparisons = Wrong Conclusions = Wrong Results. What are the wrong comparisons we need to correct if we're going to improve this company?" he thought. *I guess when we're comparing, we're really measuring. So if we use the wrong yardstick, we'll come to the wrong conclusions and get the wrong results.*

Ray took a yellow tablet out of his desk drawer, picked up his pencil, and began to write down several outdated performance measures.

1. *The monthly P&L*

It has created, he wrote, *a disease of familiarity in the company.* While it's okay for external reporting to corporate headquarters and regulatory agencies, we've proven that it hides non-value-added waste, encourages end-of-month behavior, and leads us to believe that overhead costs apply equally to every product and customer. Kathi has shown us that an ABM P&L gives us much more useful decision-making information.

Then Ray had an idea. *Maybe we should publish a simple daily P&L for all employees to see. That would encourage us to make and ship as much as we can daily. Currently we ship fifty-five percent of the product in the last week of the month. Why? Because employees procrastinate and wait until the end of the accounting month!*

2. *Classifying employees as direct and indirect*

This is an unhealthy comparison. By classifying Al's union employees as direct and the office support staff as indirect we have created a caste system. We assume that anyone classified as *direct* touches the product and therefore adds value. Conversely, we assume that anyone who is *indirect* doesn't add value. Kathi's ABM analysis has proven both of these assumptions wrong. Direct employees can perform non-value activities like *Rework Parts* and *Move Material.* And indirect employees can do value activities like *Design Products* and *Take Orders.* We should be managing activities, not the classifications of people.

3. *Time card reporting*

We've assumed that if everyone is at work, we're going to be productive. But, as we learned from Noel when we created the activity accounting spreadsheet for Receiving, "Busyness does not equal productivity." It's apparent from the ABM analysis that we should be measuring output, not time. We need to measure the outputs of departments and processes on a regular basis. Also, those project time reports that design engineers fill out each week are not as important as their output: how many prototypes did they build, or how many lines of software code did they write?

The phone interrupted his thoughts. It was Kathi. "Ray, we could use some more facilitators for the ABM continuous improvement workshops. Do you have some time this week to help?"

"Sure. What do you need me to do?"

"Call Valerie; she has the workshop schedule."

"Okay. How are things going so far?"

"You won't believe what's happened."

"Good news or bad news?"

"All I can say at this point is that I think you and the entire management team will be pleasantly surprised when you see our report next week."

"No fair. At least give me a hint," said Ray.

"Well, since you asked nicely . . . the employees we have met with so far have come up with over $1 million in cost-saving ideas. The ideas require no capital, can be approved by John, and will likely have an impact on the P&L within ninety to one hundred and twenty days."

"Outstanding! I needed some good news."

"Speaking of good news, I hear Lindsey is getting better every day."

"She sure is. Thanks for asking. In fact, she may be coming home soon."

"Wonderful," said Kathi.

"I know, I can't wait."

As soon as Ray hung up, he called Valerie. She asked him to help her lead three ABM improvement workshops that week, beginning with one that afternoon. Ray looked forward to the experience. He needed some payoff in his life. Bringing Lindsey home this weekend was the most important thing, but he was also anxious for all the hard work on ABM to begin producing results on Megna's income statement.

20

"Excuse me," Dr. Cochran said as he stepped into Lindsey's room. "I'm not interrupting anything am I?"

"No, not at all," Ray said. "Come on in." Gloria stood and said hello, while David's attention remained glued to a video game. As for Lindsey, her eyes were closed, but she wasn't asleep. She was listening to her Walkman. When Gloria tapped her on the knee, Lindsey looked up, removed her headphones, and smiled. "Hi, Dr. Cochran."

"Hey, Lindsey. How are you doing?"

"Great! When can I go home?" she asked hopefully. She had asked the same question every day since regaining consciousness. It had become something of a joke between her and the doctor.

"Well, actually, that's why I'm here," said Dr. Cochran. "All of your tests are back. I've consulted with the other doctors who've been helping us. And I've talked with your therapists. We all think you can go home first thing in the morning."

It took a moment for the news to sink in, and then Gloria started to laugh and cry at the same time. "You made it, Lindsey. You're coming home!" The room was a riot of hugs and squeals.

Ray leaned against the wall and whispered, "Thank you, God."

"Doctor, is there anything we need to watch for or be concerned about when we take Lindsey home?" Gloria asked.

"No, not really," said Dr. Cochran. "We think everything's going to be fine. She'll need to come back in about two weeks, just to make sure she's doing okay. But other than that, there's nothing else."

"That's great, doctor!" Ray shook his hand. Gloria gave him a hug and said, "We can't thank you enough."

"It's been a privilege to work with Lindsey," Dr. Cochran said. "I wish all our patients ended up this well." He told Lindsey he'd drop by to say good-bye in the morning and then left.

That night Gloria stayed up past midnight cleaning house, changing sheets, and doing laundry. Everything had piled up while Lindsey was in the hospital, but Gloria felt a new burst of energy now. She wanted the house to look great when Lindsey got home. Gloria's parents had planned to come for Thanksgiving but they had postponed their trip when Lindsey became hospitalized. Now they were scheduled to arrive tomorrow.

Lindsey checked out of the hospital Friday morning with a great send off. There were balloon bouquets and a cake the nurses had ordered. Lindsey had become everyone's pet. Everyone was thrilled she was well, but they were sorry to see her go.

Gloria fixed a turkey that night, the Thanksgiving dinner they had all missed two weeks earlier. She invited Sandy and her husband to join them, and with her parents there, it was a big group. As Ray started to offer the blessing, Lindsey asked if she could do it. Lindsey spoke a clear and simple prayer of thanksgiving while Ray blinked back tears. Nothing more needed to be said.

It was a typical Thanksgiving dinner, complete with discussions of the merits of dark versus white meat and jelly versus whole-berry cranberry sauce; they concluded that the stuffing was perfect. Ray listened while David told his grandfather a riddle. Meanwhile, Gloria was describing a recipe to her mother and Sandy, and Lindsey was helping herself to salad. It was almost as if the last two months hadn't happened. *And yet,* thought Ray, *everything's changed. And I'm thankful for that.*

The following Sunday morning seemed unusually beautiful. The sun glinted on the frosty roofs, and the sky was a bright, light blue. Gloria's parents had agreed to come to church with them, so they all piled into the minivan. When they entered the church, heads turned as people pointed out Lindsey and her family. It was impossible for the people around them not to notice their smiles and the way they held hands as they sang along with the congregation.

When the time came for the message, Ray gave each family member a note card. David started drawing a picture of a dog on his.

Rev. Owens began his sermon with a funny story that loosened everyone up. After the laughter subsided, he continued. "This morning as we come to the ninth principle in our series, we meet a man who faced a situation that was anything but funny. His name was Nehemiah. His was an incredibly difficult situation, what some would call an insurmountable problem. Let's turn now to the book of Nehemiah and take a look at his life. In it, I think we'll find some encouragement for the times when *we* face insurmountable circumstances and incredibly difficult situations."

Ray and Gloria looked at each other. Rev. Owens's words were certainly timely.

"We meet Nehemiah in chapter 1. But first a little background. About a hundred years earlier, the Jews who had been captive in Babylon were allowed to return to their homeland to rebuild Jerusalem. Their temple and most of the city had been destroyed, and rebuilding the temple was of great importance to the people of God. Progress was slow, however, and things were still a mess by the time Nehemiah came on the scene.

"Not all of the Jews had returned to Jerusalem. Many stayed where they were, in what had become a part of the Persian Empire. They had built new lives in this new land. They had families and jobs. Nehemiah fell into this category. He had a great job as a cupbearer to Artaxerxes, the Persian king. It was a prestigious job, and although it carried no power, it gave Nehemiah great influence. The king listened to him.

"One day, one of Nehemiah's brothers and some other men came from Judah to visit. They told Nehemiah about the devastation in Jerusalem. The walls were broken down, and the gates had been burned. The whole place was in ruins; the people were disgraced and discouraged.

"When Nehemiah heard these things, he sat down and wept. For several days he mourned and fasted and prayed. In his prayer he mourned their predicament and asked God's permission to go back and make things right.

"In chapter 2, Nehemiah asked for permission from the king to go back and rebuild the city. The king not only allowed him to leave, but he also helped Nehemiah make arrangements for the materials he would need. Artaxerxes even gave him a royal escort!

"So Nehemiah went to Jerusalem. After staying there three walls, he went out one night and surveyed all the damage so he would know exactly what needed to be done. The people in the city already knew, but they hadn't done anything about it. They lacked leadership, and that's what Nehemiah provided.

"He called the people together and said, 'Let's rebuild the walls.' Then he put together a plan in which everyone had a role and a responsibility. And even though he faced many obstacles, including intense opposition, he got the job done.

"The wall was completed in only fifty-two days. That in itself is remarkable, even by today's standards. After that, Nehemiah set out to reach another remarkable goal: to rebuild the people. The rest of the book of Nehemiah, from chapter 7 on, tells how he did it. I'll let you read that story yourselves.

"The entire book of Nehemiah is a classic study in leadership. It tells us how to define goals and mobilize people for action. Nehemiah also provides a classical case study on how to deal with opposition to your goals. But the thing I want us to zero in on today is the principle that Nehemiah models for us. This principle enabled him to be a great success, and it's the key to helping us overcome the obstacles and difficult circumstances we face today.

"Here's the principle: *Determine what needs to be done, and then stay focused until it is done.*"

Ray wrote down what Rev. Owens had said, but he also added his own interpretation. *Define the target and then stay on target! Until I define success and write it down, both personally and professionally, it will be impossible to hit the target.*

He thought of Lindsey's daily question, "When can I go home?" It had been a clear target, and she had never wavered from it. The mental picture he had of her in rehab when she was learning to walk again gave him an image of the determination required to stay on target. If only he could have that kind of drive, that singleness of purpose, in achieving his goals. If only he could be so sure about his own goals. What, for example, was his real goal at Megna? Hitting the annual budget? Becoming a hero? Revamping the accounting department? How could he stay on target when there seemed to be so many targets?

21

"ABM causes us to work *on* our business, not *in* our business," said Ray as he and Kathi Edwards sat down in John Brady's office. John had asked them to help prepare for the presentation of the ABM plan to the headquarters, which was scheduled for the following Tuesday. Their task was to convince CEO Josh Kaplan and CFO Larry Fredricks that ABM could help Megna achieve a ten-percent increase in profitability within ninety days. The future of the company and their jobs hung in the balance.

"That's a thought-provoking statement, Ray. What exactly do you mean?" asked John as they settled into their chairs around his small conference table.

"I've noticed that our traditional P&L statement, our balance sheet, and our departmental expense reports give us a view of the financial health of Megna Electronics that's totally different from the picture ABM gives us. Our traditional accounting reports and methods cause management to get too involved *in* the business."

"Give me an example," said John.

"Well, traditional accounting causes you to ask our managers 'What kind of supplies do you have *in* your budget?' That's an example of an *in-your-business* type of question."

"You're right and so was Vince that first day. It sounds pretty stupid now that I think about it," agreed John.

"In contrast," Kathi said, "ABM allows us to ask the same manager, 'What are you planning *on* doing with your supplies budget?' That's an *on-your-business* type of question."

"Let me see if I understand what you're both saying. You're

saying that a traditional departmental expense statement tells us how much resource we've given to a department. ABM tells us what they did with those resources. ABM shows us the activities, value, and output that consumed the supplies and other resources. Am I right?"

"You've got it, John," said Ray.

"Great. Now how can we make sure headquarters gets it?" asked John.

"I recommend we begin with the activity accounting spreadsheet." Kathi placed the order processing department's spreadsheet in front of John.

Order Processing Department	Take Orders VA	Expedite Orders NVA	Change Orders NVA	Issue Credits NVA	Answer Inquiries VA	Manage Employees VA
Salary/Fringes $460,000	$248,000	$60,000	$62,000	$67,000	$6,000	$17,000
Space 50,000	20,000	5,000	7,000	5,000	3,000	10,000
Depreciation 50,000	20,000	2,000	10,000	4,000	10,000	4,000
Supplies 30,000	10,000	2,000	10,000	3,000	1,000	4,000
Other 10,000	2,000	1,000	1,000	1,000	0	5,000
Total $600,000	$300,000	$70,000	$90,000	$80,000	$20,000	$40,000
Output Measures	10,000 Orders	1,000 Expedites	2,000 Changes	4,000 Credits	4,000 Calls	15 People
Cost per Output	$30	$70	$45	$20	$5	$2,666

"The information in this activity accounting spreadsheet is the basic foundation for ABM. When Ray wrote the words 'Manage the work, not the worker' on his greaseboard a few weeks ago, it laid the foundation for everything we have done since."

"We've come a long way since then, haven't we?" said John.

"In ways you will never imagine," said Ray happily.

Kathi continued. "The activity accounting spreadsheet is the cornerstone of an ABM system. If our management and employees don't understand the principles of ABM depicted in the spreadsheet, it will be impossible for them to grasp the uses and benefits of ABM." Kathi looked to John for confirmation.

"Right," said John. "So, let me tell you what *I* understand, then you two tell me if I'm off base. Okay?"

"All right," they said in unison.

"Well, here's how I read this report. It tells me that *Take Orders* is the most expensive value-added activity and *Change Orders* is the most expensive non-value thing they do."

"Correct so far," said Kathi.

"Based on the quantity of output, I see that the majority of the workload of the department is consumed by taking 10,000 orders. I'm not quite sure whether $30 per order is good or bad. It seems high, but I don't have any basis to make that judgment right now."

"Yes, you do," said Ray. "Use common sense. If the cost per output of an activity seems high to you, it probably contains some waste."

"Can we benchmark that activity with other companies? I imagine most other manufacturers take orders too," said John.

"Yes, we could," Kathi said, "but we'll need to find some other organizations that have implemented an activity-based cost system."

"Based on how much ABM is helping us, I bet there will be plenty of organizations implementing ABM before long," added John.

Kathi winked at Ray. They had already discussed this and come to the same conclusion.

"What else can we show them, Ray?" asked John as he returned to the Order Processing spreadsheet.

"Well, I think we can use the spreadsheet to show how ABM can improve our budgeting and strategic planning," said Ray.

"How will we do that?"

"Activity-based budgeting will work like activity accounting, but in reverse. Let me explain," said Ray. "I envision three steps to budgeting. First, John, you'll set a productivity improvement target for the company budget. Let's say you set a goal of a ten percent productivity improvement. That means that order processing will need to come up with a budget plan of $27 per order next year instead of its $30 this year."

"Great! Go on," said John.

"Second," continued Ray, "each department will have to estimate the output quantities or workloads for every activity. For example, if Chris forecasts sales to increase by ten percent next year, that doesn't necessarily mean that the number of orders will increase from 10,000 to 11,000. The order size might go up instead of the number of orders."

"So how will Order Processing develop their workload estimate?" asked John.

"By working with Chris to learn the sales plan," said Kathi. "Activity-Based Budgeting, or ABB as I call it, will encourage departmental managers to work together before they prepare and submit their budget for your approval."

"This keeps getting better and better," said John. "So then what?"

"Well, the third step is a pretty simple calculation. You multiply the cost per output target times the estimated workload. For example, if the cost per order is targeted at $27 and the predicted number of orders is 10,500, the head count and resource budget for that activity would be $283,500."

"Wait a minute," said John. "That's less than they spend today!"

"Right," said Ray. "In this example, that's what would happen. In other instances, the activity costs might go up. The real beauty of the ABB approach, John, is that departmental managers and their employees will be able to more effectively plan how they are going to achieve their budget before you review and approve it."

"And I'll be able to ask more intelligent questions during the budget reviews." John said with a grin. "Instead of asking stupid questions like 'What is your budgeted head count?' I'll be able to ask intelligent questions such as 'Why are you budgeting to take more orders next year?' or 'What plans do you have to reduce the cost of expediting?'"

"As Kathi said earlier," Ray replied, "it all starts with this simple, yet powerful, activity accounting spreadsheet."

"That's terrific, Ray. It all seems so simple. Why haven't we done it before? Hold it, you already told me. We've been working *in* our business, not *on* our business. Right?"

Ray and Kathi just smiled and nodded.

As Ray got up to get coffee for everyone, Kathi handed out the Sales Order Process report.

Sales Order Process

Department	Activity	Value	NVA	Total
Field	Visit Customers	$ 400,000		$ 400,000
Order Processing	Answer Inquiries	$ 20,000		$ 20,000
Order Processing	Take Orders	$ 300,000		$ 300,000
I.S.	Run MRP	$ 330,000		$ 330,000
A/R	Correct Errors		$ 60,000	$ 60,000
Order Processing	Change Order		$ 90,000	$ 90,000
Field	Expedite Order		$ 140,000	$ 140,000
Order Processing	Expedite Order		$ 70,000	$ 70,000
Shipping	Ship Order	$ 500,000		$ 500,000
A/R	Issue Invoice	$ 450,000		$ 450,000
Receiving	Process Return		$ 300,000	$ 300,000
Warehouse	Restock Product		$ 300,000	$ 300,000
Shipping	Reship Order		$ 200,000	$ 200,000
A/R	Reissue Invoice		$ 260,000	$ 260,000
Order Processing	Issue Credit		$ 80,000	$ 80,000
		$ 2,000,000	$ 1,500,000	$ 3,500,000
		57%	43%	

"John, this report was created using our ABM software. It will be a very useful tool."

"Okay. Take me through it."

"Well, it's actually pretty simple. We found that every activity in the company is actually a step in a business process. For example, the activity *Take Orders* is one activity or step in the *Sales Order Process*. Our ABM team defined a business process as a series of activities, which are performed by different departments to produce a common output. We found ten business processes in Megna."

"So the output of the Sales Order Process is a completed customer order?"

"Exactly," said Kathi. "As you can see, the Sales Order Process has many activities. Some add value and some non-value."

"What can we do with a report like this?" said John.

Ray explained, "I see three primary uses. First, this is a great tool to help organize process-improvement teams. One of the reasons this process has so much waste is that it's not synchronized. We'll likely need to recruit a process manager to lead the improvement effort."

"We already have a Sales Manager, Chris Meyers," said John.

"Yes, but his authority is vertical on the organizational chart. In addition to Chris, we need to define someone with horizontal authority that crosses functional boundaries. In other words, in addition to a Sales department manager we need a Sales Order Process Manager."

"Maybe we should call that person the Manager of Getting Stuff to the Customer," said Kathi, laughing.

"Not a bad idea, Kathi," said John. "What's the second use, Ray?"

"Process reports will be a great tool for budgeting. If we roll up our budgets in this fashion, we can tell if all the department managers have used the same budget improvement and workload guidelines. With Activity-Based Budgeting business process reports, we'll be able to tell if departmental budgets are synchronized or using separate assumptions." John agreed with a nod. "The third use is strategic in nature. Kathi, give John the ABM P&L."

Megna Electronics ABM P&L ($000s)	Value	Non-Value	Total
Sales	$35,000	$0	$35,000
Less: Raw Materials	9,000	1,000	10,000
Less: Procurement Process	2,000	700	2,700
Sales Order Process	2,000	1,500	3,500
Manufacturing Process	6,400	2,900	9,300
New Product Process	1,500	500	2,000
Compliance Process	1,000	500	1,500
Budgeting Process	200	400	600
Maintenance Process	500	500	1,000
Marketing Process	2,000	1,500	3,500
Management Process	390	10	400
People Process	450	50	500
Total Processes	$16,440	$8,560	$25,000
TOTAL COSTS	$25,440	$9,560	$35,000
Pre-Tax Profit	$9,560	-$9,560	$0

"The ABM P&L you are looking at reflects actual performance. We will also be able to look at our budget and strategic plans in this format."

"Give me an example of how we could use it for strategic planning," asked John.

"Well, let's take the Procurement Process for example. One question senior management should ask is, 'Have we given the Procurement Process too much or not enough resources to accomplish the strategic plan?' Notice in the ABM P&L in front of you, John, that we spent more money on Procurement than we did on New Product Introductions. This ABM report doesn't tell you whether that is a right or wrong resource decision. But it does provide you with information *on* the business that might cause us to rethink our plans and reallocate our budgeted resources."

"That's fantastic. Who would have ever thought that the simple phrase, *Manage the work, not the worker,* and a spreadsheet could provide us with so much useful information? It's truly amazing. You've both done a super job."

"Thanks, John." said Ray. "What else do you need for the presentation?"

"I'm assuming the final results of the continuous improvement workshops will be ready by next week. That's an important part of demonstrating how we're going to meet our annual profit commitment."

"We'll have it all done for you on Monday," Kathi said as she stood up to leave. "I'll round up all the workshop action plans today, Ray. Is there anything else you need from me?"

"No," said Ray, "but do make sure that you tell the entire ABM team that I expect them to participate in Monday's final run-through. I want everyone to recognize that this was truly a team effort. Besides, it's going to take a team effort to achieve and sustain the savings."

"No problem. We'll be there."

After Kathi left, Mary arrived. "Would you all like to come down and see the Continuous Improvement prize wheel?" she asked.

"Sure," said John and Ray together.

They went down to the cafeteria and admired the colorful six-foot tall wheel. "It looks great," said Ray. As he walked closer, he saw that the wheel had been sliced into approximately thirty sections, each with a prize offering listed. There was a dinner for four at a local restaurant, tickets to *The Nutcracker*, a ski weekend, and many more prizes.

"How did you do all this so quickly?" asked Ray.

"We have our ways," said Mary slyly. "John gave me the go-ahead a couple of weeks ago, and we've already given every employee who has offered improvement ideas during the ABM workshops some chips. Many have continued to turn in new ideas even after the workshops were over. I've given them chips too."

Mary turned to John. "I think your idea of kicking off the wheel program on the day headquarters is here is a great idea. They can be eyewitnesses to the results it produces. We're telling everyone to gather in the cafeteria at noon next Tuesday when they're here. Then we'll ask anyone who has at least three chips to turn them in, shake John's hand, and spin the wheel for a prize. It should be a lot of fun. And we do have reason to celebrate—there are so many great ideas that have come out of this."

John turned to Ray saying, "I suppose the hard part will be to decide which ideas to actually use."

Ray nodded. "You're right. There have been many ideas, some very creative and unique and others so obvious I can't believe we didn't think of them years ago. The temptation is to try to implement them all, and of course that's impossible. So we've tried to focus on our target, reducing costs by ten percent, and sticking with it until we get there. Each idea is evaluated on how well it will help us achieve our goal."

"And once we reach our goal?" said John.

"Then," said Ray, "in a broader sense, we need to keep the company's mission in mind. A seemingly good idea could lead us off into territory where we don't belong. We'll need to look at each idea and see how it contributes to the vision for the company, if it makes sense given the business we're in. And that applies not only to Megna's Wheel of Fortune, but to all activities we perform. We'll need to constantly ask ourselves, 'What's our business?' and then,

'How's business?' Everything we do should be measured against our mission, our strategic plan, and of course our budget."

"Our new, improved activity-based budget," added John with a grin.

Before Ray headed back to his office, John had one more request. "Ray," he said, "I'm feeling pretty confident about all this tangible evidence that ABM will help us turn this company around. But our presentation could use some theory to complement our practical findings. I think it would show how much thought has gone into this project. It would demonstrate that we're prepared to undergo significant changes in the interest of keeping Megna healthy."

"Good point," said Ray. "What do you have in mind?"

"Well," said John, "you seem to have come to some basic conclusions, truths really, about ABM. Do you think you could come up with, say, a top ten list of lessons we've learned through this process?"

"I know I can," said Ray, trying not to laugh. "I'll put it together by Monday."

As Ray walked back to his office, he wondered, *What is the tenth principle anyway? And would it change anything we've done so far?*

22

Ray had decided he needed to apply what he called "The Nehemiah Principle" to Bill. Things had not been right between them since they "had words" in Ray's office over the issue of suing the trucking company. Ray had tried to apologize for his insulting behavior, but Bill had avoided any contact. Ray saw restoring their friendship as his target, and he was determined to stay with it until Bill had forgiven him.

He persistently called and dropped by, but Bill was always unavailable. Ray had even written him a letter telling him how he felt, but there had been no reply.

In the meantime, things were going well at home. Gloria was very happy, Lindsey was back at school, and David's behavior had straightened out. And now the holiday season was underway. Christmas came at the same time every year, but it always caught Ray by surprise. Ray's focus was on getting through the next week. He'd have a few days to celebrate after that.

Gloria's parents stayed a few extra days so they could go with the family to the winter concert at David's school. David's class had been practicing their songs for weeks: "Silver Bells," "Deck the Halls," and "My Favorite Things." Ray knew them backward and forward by the time the concert came. And the concert was a big success. Ray was glad David had a chance to be in the spotlight for a change since the past few weeks had been all about Lindsey.

On Sunday the church looked especially beautiful; the sanctuary was decorated with poinsettias and evergreen garland. As a young family stood up front and lit the advent candle, Ray reflected on the last ten weeks. He leaned over and whispered to Gloria, "I will always be thankful that you found this place for us." He hated for the sermon series to end, anxious as he was to hear Principle Ten, but he knew that there would be other series and lessons to be learned. There was no reason they had to stop coming to church now that the ten weeks were up.

"The final message in our series," Rev. Owens began, "may be the most important of all. I say this because the principle we're going to learn this morning really affects all of the others. In other words, if we can master this one, we can handle all the others. However, if we mess up on this one, it's doubtful we'll have much success with the others. The reason is this: The final principle has to do with leadership. How we lead our lives affects the lives of others. What you and I say and do brings ramifications far beyond ourselves.

"Please open your Bibles and turn to Genesis, chapter 13. Here we meet two men: Abraham, a great man of faith, and Lot, his nephew. God had promised to make Abraham into a great nation, to give his descendants a land of their own. He told Abraham to leave the home he knew and go to the land of Canaan. Abraham took Lot along and as time went on, he and Lot both prospered. Eventually their flocks and herds had grown to where they had to compete for grazing land. A quarrel broke out between their herdsmen.

"Being a godly man, Abraham said to Lot, in verses 8 and 9, 'Let's not have any quarreling between you and me, or between your herdsmen and mine, for we are brothers. Is not the whole land before you? Let's part company. If you go to the left, I'll go to the right; if you go to the right, I'll go to the left.' Wouldn't it be nice if all the Christmas shoppers acted that way in the parking lot at the mall!" Everyone must have been at the mall the day before, because they all laughed.

"Well, given first choice, Lot looked up and chose the well-watered plain of the Jordan. Notice that he didn't pray about it or check out his decision with God. He just trusted what he saw with his own eyes and chose the best piece of land. So Lot and

Abraham parted and Lot 'lived among the cities of the plain and pitched his tents near Sodom.' His uncle Abraham continued to live in the land of Canaan.

"Without knowing it, Lot had made a deadly decision that would affect not only his life but the lives of his entire family. His leadership would lead his own family down a path of devastation and destruction.

"As we follow the story of his life in Genesis chapters 13 through 19, we see that things began to go downhill when he looked *toward* Sodom, a city that was known in the region for its wickedness. Next he lived *near* Sodom. Then he wanted all that the city had to offer his family, and it wasn't long until he actually lived *in* Sodom. The inevitable result? He and his family ultimately *loved* Sodom. Lot even became a leader in Sodom—the Bible tells us he had a respected position at the city gate.

"Moving near Sodom seemed like a harmless, insignificant decision at first. But it wasn't long before Lot and his family were in so deep they couldn't get out. In fact, God sent two angels to warn Lot to leave Sodom before He destroyed it. But when Lot went to warn the men who were going to marry his daughters telling them that God was about to destroy the city because of its wickedness, they thought he was kidding. You see, when he finally tried to take a stand for God, it was too late. He'd lost all credibility; his future sons-in-law thought his faith was a joke.

"Lot himself hesitated to leave Sodom. The angels had to grab him and his family by the hand to lead them out of Sodom. How tragic that the husband and father who led his family *into* Sodom didn't have the moral or spiritual strength to lead them *out* of Sodom.

"Even though the angels warned Lot and his family not to look back once they left Sodom, Lot's wife ignored their warning, looked back, and was immediately turned into a pillar of salt. And Lot and his daughters ended up living in a cave.

"Now don't miss the principle here: *Leaders must improve the lives of the people they lead.* Lot failed to do this, and it cost him everything that was dear to him. He made decisions that were good for his cattle but devastating for his kids. He got his wish to live in Sodom but lost his wife because he lived there. He paid a terrible price for being a poor leader. Sadly, he was his family's stumbling block.

"But look at Abraham's leadership. He sought to keep peace in the first place by offering Lot first choice of the land. He could do this because he trusted God to provide him with everything he needed. The result was that he, his wife, and the rest of his household prospered. Lot trusted in what he *saw*, not knowing that the well-watered plain of the Jordan would become a wasteland, Abraham trusted in things *unseen*—God and His promises.

"As we conclude this series, I hope you will think about your own leadership, whether it is at work, at school, or at home. What kind of leader are you and what kind of leader do you want to be? Who do you look to when you have important decisions to make? Fathers, I challenge you to assume the leadership of your family. Ask God to help you be the leader your family needs and deserves. Wives and children, pray that Dad will be all God wants him to be, and that he'll have the moral and spiritual courage to lead you down the right paths."

Gloria squeezed Ray's hand and whispered to him, "Thank you for being like Abraham and leading us to be a better family."

Ray had never thought of himself as a leader at home. He was a leader at work. He managed and made decisions that affected his staff. But he was awed and humbled at the idea of being the leader of his family.

Gloria had always been the one who kept the family going—planning vacations, signing the kids up for activities, making sure they all had clean clothes to wear and food to eat. She'd planned their social lives and given them jobs to do around the house. She was a great manager. But she apparently looked to *him* as the leader, and he hadn't even known it. He wasn't sure how to be a really good leader, and he wasn't sure he was up to the job, the stakes seemed so high. But then he remembered what Rev. Owens had said early in the series, "If God can use Rahab, he can use you and me."

Ray took a deep breath as he thought about his role as a husband and father. Being a leader to Gloria and Lindsey and David meant more than providing an income and security for his family.

That was easy compared to the responsibility Rev. Owens was talking about. Ray resolved to start being a strong leader using the same principles he was using at Megna. He hadn't always approached being a husband and father this way, but he could start now. He couldn't hold back a smile as he thought about how much these principles had taught him in the business world. Megna was going through some important changes as a result, and Ray knew he was experiencing those changes too. As his thoughts turned to Megna, he studied the principle on his note card.

Ray made a few notes and then paused. He couldn't see how this fit into the top ten list John had requested for tomorrow.

23

When Ray got to the office Monday morning, he took a pile of note cards from his briefcase, went straight to his greaseboard, and started writing. When Kathi came by half an hour later, she saw a nearly completed chart on the board. She stepped a little closer, reading what it said.

"This is great, Ray," she said. "Just one question. Why did you leave the last ABM principle blank?"

"Well," said Ray, "I learned the last biblical principle yesterday, and frankly I haven't figured out how it fits in here. How do we lead people here at Megna and how does our leadership improve their lives?"

Kathi thought for a moment. Then she said, "Maybe ABM helps improve the lives of the people you lead."

"What do you mean?"

"Think about it," she replied. "In order for ABM to be successful, we have to train people and to give them the tools to make it work. That improves their work, which in turn *must* improve their lives."

"That's good," said Ray, mulling it over. "And you could argue that, as leaders, if we don't choose to reap the benefits that ABM makes possible, we're responsible for the possible failure of our company, and the loss of our jobs. Even if the company survived, we'd probably cut costs by laying off employees. Those are serious consequences!"

Kathi agreed. "That must be it then," said Ray. "I knew it had to apply somehow. Thanks for figuring it out."

Bible Character	Biblical Principle	ABM Principle
Moses	Manage your own work before you try to manage others.	Manage the work, not the worker.
Rahab	The way to get your needs met is to meet the needs of others.	Identify your customers and serve their needs.
David	Focus energy on fighting the enemy, not friends and family.	Attack the competition, not each other.
Jonah	Nothing will begin to improve in your life until you are willing to make the changes necessary to improve yourself.	Don't expect improved results performing last year's activities using last year's methods.
Joseph	It's never wrong to do what's right and never right to do what's wrong.	Make sure you're doing the right thing instead of doing the wrong thing right.
Esther	The cost of solving a problem is usually less than the cost of ignoring it.	Don't kill the messenger of bad news.
Samson	You can't do the same thing over and over again expecting better results.	Don't coast—it's always downhill.
Caleb	When you make wrong comparisons you get wrong conclusions.	Eliminate unhealthy comparisons and outdated performance measures.
Nehemiah	Determine what needs to be done, and then stay with it until it's done.	Ask ourselves annually, "What's our business?" and "How's business?"
Abraham	Our leadership must improve the lives of the people we lead.	Employees will do a good job if they are given value-added activities.

"Anytime," said Kathi. "Listen, I gave John the workshop reports he needed, so I guess we're ready. Do you think headquarters will give us the go-ahead to implement the plan?"

"I can't really say," said Ray. "But the plan so clearly demonstrates how we can improve our numbers that I've got to believe they'll give us a chance. I'm just hoping that everyone will be supportive when we present it. We need to show them that everyone here is taking this seriously and will make the changes we think are necessary."

"I know what you mean," said Kathi as she went out.

A short time later, Ray got a call from Chuck Anderson asking Ray to stop by his office. Ray wondered what this was all about. He wouldn't put it past Chuck to try to throw a wrench in the plan just as they were preparing to meet with headquarters. They'd worked too hard to let Chuck's attitude wreck everything. By the time he reached Chuck's office, Ray was ready to do battle, even if it meant jeopardizing his career.

"C'mon in," said Chuck. Ray entered stiffly.

Chuck sat down and motioned for Ray to sit as well. "Ray, I wanted to thank you personally for what you've done for Megna. I know I've been hard to persuade at times, and I admire you for sticking to your guns."

Ray waited for him to say, "But," and launch into another attack.

It never came. Instead, Chuck offered to help with the presentation in any way he could and assured Ray of his complete support.

"Just know that I'm with you one hundred percent," said Chuck. "You know," he went on, "John asked me months ago to play the role of devil's advocate at staff meetings. When it seems that the momentum of everyone is heading in one direction, it's my job to jump in and present an opposing view. That way he feels we've properly considered all sides of an issue. Unfortunately, it doesn't make me a very popular guy."

Ray couldn't believe he was having this conversation. It was too weird. But before he knew what was happening, Chuck had put a wooden plaque in his hands. "This is a gift from me to you. I know it doesn't make up for the grief I gave you, but the sentiment seems right. You know I'm a big Notre Dame fan; it's a quote by their former coach, Lou Holtz."

Ray looked down and read the plaque aloud: "We are not where we want to be; we are not where we should be; we are not where we are going to be; but, thank God, we are not where we used to be."

"Yeah, thank God," said Ray, smiling. "Thanks, Chuck. Thanks a lot." Ray left in a daze. "What next?" he thought.

Back in his office, Ray finished the overhead John had requested. When he finished his Top Ten list he called Kathi in to take a look at it.

"I know it's not as clever as your Ten Commandments," he said, "but I think it sums up the main things we've learned. What do you think?"

Principles of Activity-Based Management

1. Manage the work, not the worker. Eliminating people does not eliminate the root cause of costs. Activities consume costs and products; services and customers consume activities. Address the root causes of activities to achieve sustainable improvement.
2. Define the customers of your activity and process. Determine if customers are satisfied with the cost, quality, service level, and response time of your output. Use ABM in concert with Total Quality Management, Six Sigma Business Process Reengineering, Benchmarking, and other tools to improve activities in order to meet customer's needs.
3. Attack the competition, not each other. Form crossfunctional business process teams. Define process managers. Synchronize activities across functional boundaries to create simple, mistake-proof, and flexible processes that meet customer needs.
4. Don't perform last year's activities using last year's methods and expect improved results this year. Benchmark value-added activities with the best in the world, implement improvement, and celebrate the results.
5. It is more important to do the right thing than to do wrong things right. Eliminate non-value-added wasteful activities. Optimize value and minimize waste. Obliterate, don't automate waste. Redeploy non-value resources to fund growth or improve profits.

6. Don't kill the messenger of bad news. Celebrate finding errors and root causes of activities. Do not celebrate the repetition of errors or variances to the plan. Define and resolve the root causes of unnecessary activities, excessive costs, and poor quality. Implement solutions to the root causes.
7. Don't coast—it's always downhill. Continuous improvement of activities and processes is a step-by-step uphill journey to remain competitive. ABM is not a diet. ABM is an unending process of analysis, action, and accounting.
8. Eliminate unhealthy comparisons and outdated performance measures. Disregard indirect versus direct head count statistics and other irrelevant measures. Manage activities, processes, output, and value, not the classification of employees.
9. Ask yourself annually, "What's our business?" and "How's business?" Determine if your activities and performance support the mission statement of the organization. Define activity measures necessary to achieve the mission, strategic plan, and budget.
10. Employees want to do a good job. And they will do a good job if they enjoy their job. To create this environment, leaders must provide employees with targets, training, and tools to create jobs of value-added activities.

"Wow!" said Kathi. "I think that covers it. Do I get a copy?"

"Sure," said Ray. "You get a free one since you helped."

As Ray packed up his briefcase that evening, he thought about how well the final run-through for the presentation had gone. If headquarters didn't give them a green light, it wouldn't be because they had failed to come up with a good plan. There was nothing left to do but wait until tomorrow.

There was a knock at his door just as he was putting on his coat. "Come in," he called. He turned around and saw Bill. Ray was speechless for a moment, then said, "Hey, long time no see."

"Yeah," said Bill. "I just wanted to drop by and tell you good luck tomorrow."

"Thanks," said Ray.

"You know, you've done a great thing for the company and I'm proud to be your friend," said Bill, looking at the floor.

"Does that mean you've forgiven me for the things I said?" asked Ray.

"Yeah," said Bill softly. Then he grinned. "But don't expect me to cut you any slack on the golf course." And then he was gone.

"Doesn't that beat all," thought Ray, glancing at the Nehemiah principle on his greaseboard before he turned off the lights and shut the door.

24

Josh Kaplan and Larry Fredricks, "the headquarters guys," came with John to Ray's office late on Tuesday afternoon. They had spent the whole day at Megna, starting with the presentation in the conference room. They had watched the Wheel of Fortune's inaugural spin in the cafeteria and eaten lunch there. Later they toured the plant, poured over spreadsheets and reports, and met privately with John in his office.

They had asked good questions in the presentation and seemed satisfied with the answers given. Ray was pleased at how quickly they had grasped the basic concept of ABM and was sure they understood its most important uses. However, they hadn't given the nod yet. Everyone was on pins and needles. No one wanted to go home until they knew what the outcome of this visit would be.

"Ray, may we come in?" John asked.

"Of course," said Ray, his heart pounding. He stood up to shake hands with Josh and Larry and offered them a seat.

"Ray," began Josh, "we've been very impressed by what we've seen here today. We've been discussing Megna's future with John. He has made it clear that you are the brains behind this ABM plan."

"Well," said Ray, "it truly has been a team effort. Everyone has worked very hard, and good ideas have come from all departments."

"We understand that," said Josh, "but we also understand that it usually takes one big idea to make the others happen, and John tells us that you not only came up with the big idea but also managed the project from start to finish. And we also know that you did it all while you were under a great deal of personal stress. We just want you to know that we're aware of your contribution and that we appreciate it."

"Thank you," said Ray. "It's been a privilege to be involved."

"What we want to know, Ray, is how you might feel about working someplace else."

Ray looked wildly at John. "Are we out of a job then, John?"

John started to laugh. "No, Ray. Josh and Larry are satisfied that we can increase our profits with the ABM plan. They've given us the okay to implement it."

Larry broke in. "Ray, it's just that the plan is so good, we'd like to try it in other divisions. But we don't want to reinvent the wheel. We need an expert like you to help us."

"You don't need to let us know now, Ray," said Josh. "Take some time with your family. Enjoy the holidays, and then if you're interested, come talk to us after the New Year."

After they left, Ray called Gloria to tell her that the plan had been approved. He decided to wait to tell her about the other news. "I'm coming home now," he said.

He could tell that news of headquarters' approval had spread. He could hear whoops and cheers up and down the halls. Kathi came by on her way out. "We did it, Ray!"

"Indeed, we did," said Ray. "And we couldn't have done it without you. You're a star."

Ray thought he should recommend Kathi to Josh and Larry. "Well," said Kathi, "it's great to work for a boss like you."

"Wait a second and I'll walk out with you," said Ray. He said good-bye to Kathi in the parking lot and then headed for home in time to have dinner with his family.

25

Ray stood by the window, staring out at the lighted street. He was the only one awake to enjoy the sight. The neighborhood had put on quite a light show for the holiday season this year. Now that the holidays had passed, it wouldn't be long before the flashing and fading bulbs were put away. He'd miss them; this was a yearly activity for him. He always spent time studying the lights as he considered the new year and what it might hold.

It had been a quiet but wonderful Christmas this year. Having Lindsey walking and nearly recovered had been the best present of all. He had savored the time with his family and been more involved with the holidays and fun than many past Christmases. He had avoided thinking about what Josh and Larry had said until Christmas was over in order to make the most of the time with his family. But it was time to consider the job opportunity he had been given, as the holidays were now over.

Gloria had given him her full support, even if it meant moving, and he knew she meant it. They had discussed both options thoroughly. Ray had even called his boss and talked things over with John Brady for some more perspective. He wanted to do the right thing for everyone involved: his family, Megna, himself. John was encouraging and also supported whatever decision he came to; though he would be sorry to lose Ray, he knew having him working at headquarters would mean Megna would benefit from his work.

Staying in his current job seemed so safe and yet so exciting. He wanted to be there when the ABM plan really started to work.

It was his project, and not being there to see and experience the full results didn't feel like the right thing to do. And he wasn't comfortable with the idea of going somewhere new, of having to prove himself again and having to make new friends. Yet the potential for expanding ABM to other divisions and perhaps corporations was too big to ignore. Changing jobs represented an opportunity to really add his mark to the business world, but he didn't want to leave the rest of his life, his family, out of the decision either.

He had thought a lot about what Rev. Owens said about leading his family, and he wondered how working for headquarters would affect them all. It was so confusing to consider how such a change would affect life as they knew it.

Ray thought that perhaps Rev. Owens could give him some guidance on his job dilemma, so he had met with him earlier in the week. During their visit, Rev. Owens let him talk everything out. They spent a long time talking, with Ray asking hard questions and Rev. Owens giving honest answers.

Through it all, Ray found there was an issue more pressing than his business interests, one that he no longer wanted to ignore. Rev. Owens prayed with him and recommended that Ray read the Bible on his own. He gave Ray ideas of books in the Bible to start with. Some had been covered in the sermon series, and others were new to Ray, like John and Matthew.

Ray had taken Rev. Owens's advice and read, prayed, and thought a lot since then. It had led him to an important conclusion. He wanted God to lead his life. Ray knew that by taking this step, life as he knew it would change. But by now, he was convinced that it would be a good change, something he'd needed to do all along. He wasn't sure where this move would lead, but he trusted it would be in the right direction. He just knew it was the right thing to do, whatever the outcome of his job dilemma.

Gloria, too, was considering how God fit into her life. Both she and Ray acknowledged that Lindsey's accident had shown them clearly how little control they had over their lives. Rev. Owens had prayed with both of them, and now all three were praying for Lindsey and David as well. It was an exciting time for the Miller family.

Ray breathed a peaceful sigh as he considered his new commitment. The future and his job considerations were manageable. Even on the night before he announced his decision, he felt calm. Whether he stayed at Megna in Accounting or changed over to headquarters, things were going to be different, and better. He smiled to himself, thinking about how much had changed in just three months, and also for the changes to come. He wasn't worried about what he should do anymore, however. He knew everything would work out, because he knew where he was headed.

Epilogue

Ray studied the charts on his desk with delight. Megna Electronics was thriving, thanks to Activity-Based Cost Management. Kathi faithfully sent over spreadsheets to demonstrate how far the company had come. She had taken over his position six months before when he began working for headquarters, and the two still talked on a regular basis as she learned the ropes and they compared notes on how ABM was working. Ray missed his team but enjoyed seeing how Kathi was sustaining and improving ABM for Megna. And he knew he'd made the right decision. Progress was being made in all directions, and he loved his work.

It was a good feeling knowing he had played an important role in taking Megna Electronics from a survival mode to success. Now he was responsible for adding ABM to all divisions, including headquarters. He enjoyed the daily challenge of explaining the ten principles and systematizing the ABM style of management. He was seeing positive results in every organization, especially Megna. Change wasn't easy, but the common sense principles of ABM gave him confidence to see it through. ABM is about continuous improvement and performance measurement. ABC is all about improved decision-making. And now he was investigating ABB . . . Activity-Based Budgeting. No matter the acronym, it is about utilizing principles that make people, families, and businesses more successful.

Ray knew there would be ups and downs in the future, but he was at peace with the future. While he was still smiling over

Megna's spreadsheets, Ray's secretary buzzed in to tell him "Your daughter Lindsey is on the phone for you."

"Dad?"

"Hi Lindsey. What's up?" Ray asked.

"Mom wants to know when you're coming home so she can start dinner." Lindsey replied.

"Well, honey, tell Mom to start right now because I'm on my way."

For additional information

on Activity Based Management . . .

You may contact Tom Pryor at:
www.ICMS.net
or
817.483.6511
or
TomPryor@icms.net

You may also contact Barry Cameron at:
www.crossroadschristian.net
or
Crossroads Christian Church
5200 South Bowen Rd.
Arlington, TX 76017
or
817.557.2277

To receive the CCC WEEKLY (a free e-mail newsletter)
Email: ccc@crossroadschristian.net

For additional resources by Barry L. Cameron, contact:
info@thedicipleshop.com
or
888.360.7648